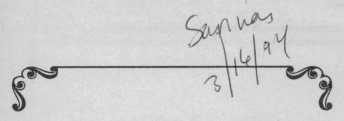

Like stars, the lamplight was reflected in her eyes, and as he looked into them, she smiled tremulously.

Raven could no more resist that smile than he could fly. As if by their own volition, his arms closed about her, drawing her close. "Elisande," he whispered, as her lips lifted to his.

Once again Elisande felt the world slide away. Warm shudders ran through her veins as she felt the passionate stroking of Lord Raven's mouth. Incredible sensations filled her, so that she seemed to be lifted from the earth and rising toward the sky.

LADY IN SHADOW

Rebecca Ward

FAWCETT CREST • NEW YORK

A Fawcett Crest Book
Published by Ballantine Books
Copyright © 1994 by Maureen Wartski

Library of Congress Catalog Card Number: 93-90719

ISBN 0-449-22225-X

Manufactured in the United States of America

First Edition: March 1994

Acknowledgment:

With thanks to Jill Marcum for her expertise and help in matters concerning the tarot.

Chapter One

"I beg you will not go out today, Lisa."

Elisande paused in the act of settling her bonnet by the small glass that had taken the place of the old ivory mirror.

"Why, Con?"

"I'm afraid something dreadful is about to occur." The small, mouse brown lady in the wing chair sighed so deeply that the scanty lace on her cap quivered like the antennae of a beetle. "Look at these cards. They *never* lie."

She gestured toward the tarot cards spread out before her on the morning-room table. "So many swords *and* the Lightning Struck Tower. Elisande, they foretell conflict, destruction, violence, and collapse!"

"Do they?" Elisande smiled faintly. "Well, forewarned is forearmed as they say."

"Elisande, this is no laughing matter!"

"I am not laughing, really. Dear Con, the cards are retelling our family history, not prophesying the future. Now, I must go or I'll be late for my meeting with Lady Carme."

Miss Constance Dayton reached out to catch her younger cousin's arm. "I wish you would not go," she said in her gruff little voice. "I remember Lady Carme from the season that I spent in London with Mama and dear Aunt Hortense. She was Laetitia Bladding then. I was very young, but I recall Miss

Bladding being green-jealous of Aunt Hortense's good looks. Sour apples don't sweeten with age, Elisande. I mislike your being in servitude to that female."

"Becoming a governess is not really 'being in servitude,' " Elisande pointed out. "Besides, Lady Carme may have changed for the better. Collect that she wrote quite civilly in answer to my letter and said that I might come and see her."

She tried to withdraw her arm, but Miss Dayton would not let her go. "Nigel will loathe what you are doing."

"He had the nightmare again last night, Con." Gravely Elisande looked down into her cousin's troubled face. "Parse couldn't calm him. When I went to help, he cried like a baby in my arms."

Her hazel eyes were dark with the memory; her clear voice had gone suddenly husky. " 'Why can't I remember?' he kept asking. 'What is going to happen to me if I can't remember?' "

"I heard him cry out." Miss Dayton batted short, stubby eyelashes against tears and said even more gruffly, "Perhaps his old wounds are hurting again. Dr. Goode must—"

"We cannot call the doctor. We owe him too much money already." Gently disengaging herself, Elisande gave her cousin's hand a pat. "I must go. Don't be so down pin, dear. I'll be back in time for a cose and a cup of your delicious rose-and-cinnamon tea. No doubt Lady Carme is probably far nicer than you remember."

The house was silent, but the ghost of a cheerful ticking followed Elisande down the stairs and to the front door. It was only a memory, for the grandfather clock on the staircase landing had been sold long ago. So had the paintings that had hung on the wall, the library of beloved books, and the statue by John Cheere that had stood in the corner now barren ex-

2

cept for Nigel's fishing pole and riding crop. The one was useless since the Reddings possessed no horses, but the other was a necessity—Nigel's skill with rod and reel as well as Parse's rabbit traps produced most of their meals.

Where was her younger brother now? Elisande wondered. She could hear or see no sign of him, nor of Parse either. Perhaps the onetime batman turned valet and man of all work had accompanied his master to the village. Or perhaps Nigel had gone for a walk in the woods. He often wanted to be alone after one of his restless nights.

What is going to happen to me if I can't remember?

Hastily Elisande walked out of the door. The morning sun had disappeared behind clouds, but mid-September heat still clung to the Sussex countryside. As she walked briskly along, skirting the village in favor of the open road, Elisande wished that her one good walking-out dress was made of lighter material. It was a three-mile trudge to Carme House, and it would never do to arrive damp and bedraggled for her interview with Lady Carme.

"I wonder what her ladyship will be like?" she murmured.

When Parse had brought home the news— gleaned while buying flour in the village—that a Lord Carme had bought the old Harrison House and that his lady was looking for a governess for her younger children, it had seemed a heaven-sent opportunity to augment the family's meager funds. Without telling the others, Elisande had written to Lady Carme, and my lady had written back agreeing to an interview. She had also added that she had known Lady Hortense Dayton, Elisande's late mother, before her marriage.

Elated, Elisande had shared this news with her

cousin, but Constance's reaction had been so negative that she had not told Nigel. "Time enough to tell him when I have the position," Elisande mused aloud. "Then I will be able to assure him that Lady Carme is not the griffin Con makes her out to be."

But her first sight of Lady Carme's residence was not reassuring. More impressed with itself than impressive, the large, square house gloomed over a garden that had been clipped and pruned to within an inch of its life. The marble lions on either side of the stairs looked stifled, and the footman who answered the huge front door had a wooden look.

With outward composure Elisande presented her card. "Miss Redding to see Lady Carme," she announced.

The footman went away, and Elisande looked around at too much dark furniture, a crowd of marble busts, and a veritable army of dour portraits.

"You won't like it here. Get out while you can," a voice whispered in her mind, but she dismissed this cowardly impulse as the footman reappeared.

"Please to come this way, miss."

As Elisande followed him up the stairs, she could hear the rise and fall of voices from a room on the first floor. These grew louder as the footman knocked on a door on the first floor, opened it, and announced, "Miss Redding, m'lady."

Seated next to an overpowering arrangement of late summer dahlias, Lady Carme seemed at first glance to be as overblown as the flowers. Flounces of cream-and-red-striped tarlatan, gingery curls surrounding a small, petulant face—Elisande's heart sank as she curtsied. It continued to sink still further as my lady raised her lorgnette to survey her visitor before extending a mere two fingers of her hand.

"So you are Hortense's daughter," she said in a breathless little voice. "I do not see the resemblance. Hortense Dayton, Lord Raven, was a beauty."

This last was addressed to a gentleman who was leaning against the marble mantelpiece in an attitude of extreme ennui. Elisande had not noticed him as she entered, but now she wondered how she could have missed him. He was above average height with fair hair cut in the popular windswept style, and he was dressed in the kick of fashion. But the face above the well-fitting gray riding coat, fawn breeches and waistcoat embroidered with silver thread was no dandy's. Hard-featured, hawknosed, burned almost mahogany by the sun, it seemed out of place in a lady's drawing room.

Disinterested blue eyes flicked over her, and Elisande felt herself being assessed, measured, and dismissed all in one second. *Rag-mannered*, she thought indignantly and then recollected why she was there. No aristocrat would consider a mere governess worthy of more than a passing glance.

"Indeed," Lady Carme was saying, "Hortense Dayton was a nonpareil with her long golden hair and green eyes. *You*, miss, do not have her coloring."

"I have been told I favor my father," Elisande said equably. "You were kind enough to answer my letter, ma'am. Might I meet the children?"

The gentleman spoke for the first time. "I'll take my leave, Lady Carme. My message has been delivered, and I must be on my way to Dorset."

His voice, Elisande noted, was as bored as his expression. He was obviously eager to be gone, just as Lady Carme was obviously anxious to keep him where he was.

Her ladyship extended a plump, beringed hand as if to physically hold him back while cooing, "No, stay, Lord Raven. After your kindness in interrupting your journey to bring me dear Anabelle's greetings, I must at least offer you some refreshment. Besides, I must pen a letter for you to take to her. This interview will soon be over."

She swiveled back to Elisande and spoke in quite a different tone. "You will meet Enid and Fiona afterward—*if* all is satisfactory."

"I understand," Elisande said. She tried to ignore Lord Raven, who had turned his back and was looking out of the window. "No doubt you have questions to ask me, ma'am."

My lady did not deign to reply at once. Since the former governess had been packed off last week in disgrace, she needed a replacement. Elisande Redding seemed a likely candidate. Though undoubtedly handsome with that wealth of chestnut hair and peach-bloom skin, she was not in her first youth—twenty-six if she was a day, Lady Carme conjectured meanly—and though her hazel eyes were clear and large and thickly starred with dark lashes, they were too direct to be appealing.

In short, Miss Redding did not possess the fragile prettiness that might tempt eighteen-year-old Percy—unfortunately sent down from Oxford over a mere boyish prank—to commit Another Indiscretion. Moreover the thought of employing Hortense Dayton's daughter was too delicious to forgo.

Elisande watched Lady Carme suck in her cheeks as though tasting something sweet before announcing, "Very well. If the children like you and Lord Carme approves, you will do. However, one thing must be made clear."

Lady Carme leaned forward. "Your brother is not to set foot on my property for any reason. I cannot abide the thought of being anywhere near a traitor."

Elisande felt as if she had been slapped in the face. Lady Carme continued, "Actually, he was doubly a traitor. Captain Redding was a trusted aide to

6

Colonel Hanard when he sold those military dispatches to the French."

"None of this is true," Elisande protested indignantly. "The military tribunal did not find Nigel guilty of any wrongdoing."

"Tol rol—he wasn't found innocent, either. 'Inconclusive evidence,' indeed."

Elisande clenched her hands at her sides but managed to speak calmly. "On the night those secrets were stolen, Nigel was beaten near to death. He must have surprised the real villains at their work."

"That was not what I heard from my dear friend Lady Anabelle Graymount—Mrs. Colonel Hanard, I should say. I had it from her that one of the military dispatches did not fall into the hands of the enemy. *That* one was found in your brother's pocket. No doubt," Lady Carme added with malicious satisfaction, "Redding demanded more money and the Frenchmen turned on him."

"How dare you malign Nigel with such lies?"

Lady Carme's eyes narrowed. "Do not use that tone with me, miss," she snapped. "You know as well as I that only Captain Redding's convenient loss of memory kept him from the hangman's noose." She paused to watch the effect of this statement on her victim before adding, "But I am persuaded he'll not avoid justice. Sooner or later he'll turn back to crime like a dog returning to his own vomit."

"An interesting analogy, that."

Both Elisande and my lady had forgotten Lord Raven, who had turned from the window and was watching them dispassionately. "Actually dogs don't in the least resemble mankind. They neither commit crimes nor indulge in gossip."

My lady bit her lip. In her just indignation, she had forgotten that Lord Raven was listening, and her lush bosom swelled with ire toward the chit who might have made her appear less than perfect in his lordship's eyes. But as she readied herself to deliver a stinging set down, Lady Carme saw that the impertinent hussy was walking toward the door.

"Wait," she commanded. "I've not done with you."

"But I have done with you." Elisande's voice shook with anger. "Good day, Lady Carme."

As she exited the room, she found the footman standing suspiciously near the door. Elisande suspected that he'd had his ear glued to the keyhole and would no doubt regale the staff below stairs with what he had heard. I should have listened to Con, she thought bitterly as she walked down the stairs and out of the door.

But humiliation was not the worst problem that the Reddings faced. "What will we do for money now?" Elisande wondered.

There was no money—had not been for some time. Papa—dear, unworldly Papa—had made unlucky speculations and left them debt-ridden at the time of his death, and Mama had used what was left to buy Nigel's commission in the Guards. Here the Reddings' luck had seemed to turn, for Colonel Hanard selected Nigel to be his aide.

Elisande's heart ached when she remembered how happy her brother had been during that time and how his letters home had glowed with hero-worship for the colonel and devotion for the colonel's daughter. To Elisande Nigel had shyly confided that Miss Sylvia Hanard returned his love and that he hoped to distinguish himself on the battlefield so as to win her hand. And then Mama had become so ill and her terrible, long illness had bled the family dry.

They had gradually let the servants go and sold

what they could—even the books that Papa had left to Elisande's special care. Nigel had wanted to sell his colors, but Mama had forbidden that, saying that he would bring the family honor and glory as a soldier—

"You bloody swine!"

The indignant shout broke sharply into Elisande's thoughts. In her preoccupation she had taken the wrong turn in the road and was nearing the village instead of her home. And that presented another problem. They had not paid the butcher for the leg of lamb bought a month ago, and he might create an unpleasant scene.

Should she retrace her steps? But several people had already seen her and it would look as if she were running away. Stiffening her spine, Elisande had begun to walk forward when the doors of the village tavern burst open disgorging several burly individuals.

They were surrounding a familiar, slender, fair-haired figure. "Oh, Lord," Elisande exclaimed in horror. "Nigel!"

What was Nigel doing at the Silver Dragon? And where was Parse? As she looked around vainly for her brother's manservant, she heard Nigel shout, "I'll draw your claret, you bloody liar."

His voice was drowned out by gleeful yells of, "A mill!" and Elisande was shouldered aside as villagers hurried over to watch the fun.

"Kill me, will yer?" A hulking lout swaggered forward, shoved his face inches away from Nigel's, and taunted, "Ow will yer do that, Sir Turncoat?"

"Like *this*!"

Nigel let fly with his fist, but before it could connect, his opponent grasped the young man's arm and twisted it.

"Like *this*, hey?"

9

There were roars of laughter as the lout punched Nigel in the stomach, then in the face. "Like *this*?"

"Stop it," Elisande screamed as several other ruffians commenced beating her brother. She tried to press through the throng of onlookers but was pushed back. "I beg you, help my brother," she pleaded to a stout villager who stood beside her, but he only snarled that it served the bloody traitor right.

Pushing and shoving, Elisande managed to make her way to the center of the crowd where the ruffians were still battering Nigel. She flung herself on their leader's back, but he shoved her aside. "You brute," she shouted, "you unspeakable bully—he's not well. You'll kill him. Cowards, to attack five against one!"

"I agree with the lady."

A gentleman had stopped the matched grays that drew his curricle and was eyeing the melee with a frown. Elisande recognized Lord Raven, but before she could entreat his help, he had dismounted and was striding over to the combatants.

"Gerrout of it, you," snarled the big brute who had started the fight, then yelped with pain as Lord Raven knocked him sprawling.

"Jackals and maggots." Laying about him with his riding crop, Lord Raven pushed himself between Elisande and the ruffians. "Get out of my way, the lot of you, before I lose my temper."

There was such menace in those deep tones that the crowd silently melted away. Nigel's adversaries, including the big ruffian who was clutching his bleeding nose, beat a hasty retreat. Meanwhile, Nigel himself fell on his knees in the dust. Elisande knelt beside him.

"How badly did they hurt you?" she cried.

He looked up at the sound of her voice. "Lisa," he

slurred. "Wha're you doing here? Shouldn't be here. No place for a lady."

There was the unmistakable smell of brandy on his breath. Nigel had been drinking. Dr. Goode had expressly forbidden alcohol, and besides, spirits cost money! But that could wait. Elisande looked up at Lord Raven and saw him regarding her with an odd expression in his blue eyes.

Pity or distaste she could not tell, but both were equally detestable. "Thank you for your assistance," she told him stiffly. "We can manage very well, now, sir."

"R-rag-mannered, that!" Nigel hiccuped. "Can't dismiss a gentleman like a lackey, dash it!" He lifted his pale face to add, "Very grateful for your assistance, sir. Blackguards attacked me in a pack—"

"Rats generally do." Lord Raven replied. He tapped his riding crop against his thigh as he asked, "Are you badly hurt?"

"No, not a bit of it. Forgetting m'manners—name's Nigel Redding. Command me in anything, sir." Nigel put his arm around Elisande's shoulder and attempted to stand, but his knees buckled under him. "Can't seem to find m'footing," he mumbled.

Lord Raven extended a nattily gloved hand and easily drew Nigel to his feet. "Allow me to help you to your carriage," he said to Elisande.

"There is no need. I can—"

"*Is* there a carriage?" Elisande shook her head. "Then we'll take my curricle."

"Not necessary," Nigel protested. "Can make m'own way home."

Paying no attention to the young man, Lord Raven commenced to half walk, half carry him toward his curricle. "We'll have to hold him up between us," he told Elisande. When she hesitated he added, "I don't know what your direction is, but your brother's in no condition to walk."

His blunt tone was completely matter of fact. In the face of common sense, Elisande put aside humiliation. "You are right," she said. "I would be most obliged to you, sir."

"See here, dash it—" but Lord Raven was already lifting Nigel into the curricle.

"Be easy, Redding," he said quietly. "No wonder you couldn't take on that rabble. I couldn't manage either, if I were in my cups. Now to get you home."

As he helped her mount, Elisande felt a mixed froth of emotions. She was thankful to Lord Raven for the civil way in which he spoke to Nigel. After having heard what Lady Carme had to say, most gentlemen would have turned their backs on the Reddings.

But gratitude did not make his company easier to bear. The fact that Lord Raven had been witness to that humiliating scene at Lady Carme's made Elisande writhe. She remained tensely silent until Lord Raven said, "He's fallen asleep, but he doesn't look well. Has he been sick?"

"He will be all right."

Elisande's tone invited no further talk, but Lord Raven continued, "Brandy's not good for a sick man."

"I'm well aware of it."

Meaning that none of this was his business. Lord Raven glanced at the slender figure standing beside him and experienced the same stir of admiration he had felt earlier when Miss Redding had walked out of Lady Carme's parlor.

In spite of the fact that her dress was covered with dust, Miss Redding held herself as straight as a lance. Her hair, which was also silvered with dust, had come free of her ancient relic of a bonnet and floated free like a chestnut halo, and her remarkable eyes were very bright and determined to ask no quarter.

The girl had spirit and address—and from what the spiteful bitch he had just left had said, Miss Redding had need of both. But, Lord Raven reminded himself, that was *not* his problem. He was, after all, facing a mare's nest of his own.

"You have the right of it," he said in an indifferent tone. "I should mind my own affairs."

Elisande glanced up at him uncertainly. "I did not mean to be rude," she said in a low tone. "I only meant that you need not be concerned about us."

Lord Raven did not answer. Nigel snored in his drunken slumber. Elisande's cheeks felt hot, and she kept her eyes steadily on the road. Now, thank heavens, she could see the house in the distance.

"Do you believe in fate, Miss Redding?" Lord Raven asked suddenly.

"I beg your pardon?"

"In some parts of the world it's believed that destiny links certain people together," his lordship said. "I've never heard of you or your brother before this. You reside in Sussex, and I have only recently returned to my estate in Scotland. And yet we share a connection of sorts."

Elisande had no idea what Lord Raven was talking about. "Indeed?" she murmured.

"Indeed. Your brother used to be Colonel Hanard's aide, and I am on my way to a wedding at Hanard House."

She turned to look up at him wide eyed. "A wedding? Whose?"

"My elder brother is marrying Miss Sylvia Hanard. Rather a remarkable coincidence, don't you think?"

Miss Hanard was getting married! Elisande had never met the colonel's daughter, but Nigel had uttered such poetic descriptions of that lady that she could picture her to the last red-gold hair.

"Of course—the newspapers would have carried the news," she murmured aloud.

Nigel may have forgotten everything that had happened at Hanard House that fateful night, but he had never faltered in his blind devotion to Sylvia Hanard. If he had learned about her marriage, it was no wonder he had become foxed.

Elisande felt a small, sick knot form under her breastbone at the thought of Nigel's suffering. "I wish your brother happy, sir," she managed to say. "Miss Hanard is said to be very beautiful."

"No doubt." It seemed to Elisande that Lord Raven's mouth tightened. But his tone was as bored as ever as he continued, "My new in-laws are the reason I am in Sussex. Colonel Hanard's second wife is a friend of Lady Carme's. Since I had business in the area, she requested that I stop and deliver a letter to that lady. Another coincidence, perhaps?"

But Elisande hardly heard him. She was thinking that Constance's tarot cards had told the truth today. Violence and catastrophe had befallen the Reddings—and the day was not over yet.

Poor Nigel, she thought. It was all so unfair—how much more pain could one man endure?

She was grateful when at last they reached the house. Parse ran out to help his master from Lord Raven's curricle, and after thanking his lordship, Elisande hastened into the house. Here she found Parse bathing Nigel's face with cool water meanwhile scolding and soothing in the same breath.

"Nay, and haven't I allus said that tha was to take me along when tha went to that there village?" the big Yorkshireman was moaning. "They'st mawworms there that do believe that muck about tha being a traitor."

He paused as Nigel turned restlessly in his sleep

and crooned, "It's all right, Captain, sir—tha'rt safe an' all. Yet t'go t'that village with thy wounds only half-healed—happen those devils at t'tavern could have punched thee silly."

He looked up as Elisande came into the room. "Miss Lisa, 'twas my fault that t'captain was at t'village alone. Soon after I brought him his newspaper this afternoon, he disappeared and I did not know where he had gone."

Elisande had already found the crumpled newspaper where Nigel had flung it. As she had suspected, there was an announcement of Miss Sylvia Hanard's coming marriage to Wigram Raven, Marquess Tanner.

"Miss Lisa, I'm fair flummoxed with worry about t'captain." Parse lowered his voice. "Today I found him with his service pistol in his hand."

Elisande felt as if every drop of her blood was draining away. "His *pistol*," she whispered. "Oh, he wouldn't—what did he say?"

"He *said* that he was cleaning it." Parse's lumpy countenance was dark with frustration and misery as he added, "I dunnot know what to do, Miss Lisa. Nay, I'd give my life for Captain Redding any day, but I dunnot know what t'do t'help him."

He broke off as Nigel gave a deep sigh. "He's waking up," Elisande warned, but Nigel's eyes remained closed.

"Shadows," he muttered. "The world is all in shadow. God, *why* can't I see more clearly?"

He was dreaming again. With her eyes on her brother's flushed face, Elisande said. "It has been nearly a year and a half since that night, and yet he cannot remember what happened. He needs to be certain in his own heart that he is not a traitor. Otherwise it will get worse and worse and in the end—"

They were both silent, thinking of Nigel with his

pistol in his hand. At last, Parse drew the back of his big hand across moist eyes. "Aye, Miss Lisa. But how is he to remember? I cannot see it, any road."

He'll return to crime like a dog returning to its vomit.

"There may be a way," Elisande said, slowly. "If we were to go to Dorset and visit Colonel Hanard's house, the shock may jar Nigel's memory."

Parse's small eyes seemed ready to pop out of their sockets. "Art daft, Miss Lisa?" he gasped. "Begging your pardon, ma'am, but we can't go *there*. Nay, it'd kill t'captain for certain."

Not going there might kill him, too. With her eyes on her brother's white face, Elisande made her decision. "Start packing, Parse, if you please," she said. "We are all going to a wedding."

Chapter Two

"Oh, what can be taking Nigel so long?"

Twisting her stubby little hands in their much-mended gloves, Constance Dayton glanced nervously at the inn door.

"He is probably inspecting our rooms and will be out in a moment." Hoping for a glimpse of her brother, Elisande looked about the courtyard of the Gilded Stag. The sight was not reassuring. All about the Reddings' hired hackney clustered horses, landaulets, carriages, traps, and various other conveyances.

Constance eyed them doubtfully. "Perhaps there are no rooms," she said gruffly. "Collect, Elisande, that when I laid out my cards this morning, I constantly drew the Moon card. And that means—"

"Here is Nigel now," Elisande interrupted, but her heart sank at the expression on his face and it took an effort to sound cheerful as she queried, "What luck?"

"None. Rooms are all bespoke for the night" was the curt reply.

"As I said, I drew the Moon card, which signifies the dark side," Constance sighed. "Wicked things belong to the dark. I'm persuaded that we should have stayed in Sussex."

Elisande spoke with a confidence she did not feel. "We will find another inn. Nigel, you know the area and can tell our driver where to go."

But her brother shook his head. "No use, Lisa. The landlord said that all the inns hereabouts are filled to overflowing. There's a prizefight on Saturday at Allford as well as the—as well as the festivities at Hanard House."

Elisande felt a surge of dismay. There was no doubt that, without her urging, the Reddings would have stayed in Sussex. She alone had been the driving force that had reasoned, coaxed, and finally goaded Nigel into making the journey.

"I believe the answers are at Hanard House," Elisande had persisted. "Don't you *want* to know what really happened the night of March thirtieth?" Then, when Nigel remained unconvinced, she had added, "Besides, if you go to Dorset you will see Miss Hanard again."

"See her given in marriage to another man, you mean," Nigel had shot back. "That's more than flesh and blood can stand."

But the lure of seeing his beloved had swung the balance, and Nigel was here now, staring down at her in the inn courtyard saying, "It's no use. We might as well take the hackney back to Allford and wait for a stage home. Parse will—but what the devil's Parse doing?"

The big Yorkshireman was standing some distance away, deep in conversation with a woman dressed in a black dress and bonnet. Now she reached out and touched Parse's arm persuasively.

"What's this?" Nigel accused as the big Yorkshireman broke off his conversation and came plodding over to his employer's side. "This is no time to be throwing the hatchet at some female."

"Nay, I wasn't doing any such thing," Parse retorted indignantly. "That there's Kate Willoughby, what was married to Sam, t' village carpenter. Happen tha remembers him, Captain?" Nigel shook his head impatiently. "Any road, Sam and me knew each other afore he went and got hisself killed at Waterloo."

Nigel winced. Elisande said hurriedly, "We are sorry for Mrs. Willoughby's loss, Parse."

"So'm I—but that's not what I'm driving at. Kate says that after Sam piked away, she's hated living in t'new cottage he built for her in t'village. Too big for her, she said, with too many memories. Any road, she's been thinking on going t'live wi' her old mother some doors down, so she's willing to let t'cottage to us."

"Would she?" Elisande exclaimed. "How wonderfully fortunate! It seems the answer to our prayers."

She started to step down from the hackney, but Nigel stopped her. "Not a good idea, Lisa," he said in a low tone. "Willoughby was killed at Waterloo, Parse said."

Meaning that a traitor would not find welcome in a hero's house—Elisande thrust away that dark thought and said stoutly, "We have traveled an entire day and a night to come here. Let's at least hear what she has to say."

Under her severe black bonnet, Mrs. Willoughby turned out to be a plump, pretty person with soft brown hair and even softer brown eyes. With many helpless glances and gestures she reiterated that she would be grateful for tenants.

"I'm all alone in the world, sir and ma'am," she sighed, "and as I was telling Mr. Parse just now, my daughter and me are lonely all alone in that cottage. It may be a poor place to such as yourselves, but it's big for 'Arriet and me and that pretty. My man fixed it up fine before 'e went to war and got 'isself kilt."

She dabbed her eyes with the edge of her apron but recovered immediately when Elisande asked to see the cottage. "Come right this way," Mrs.

Willoughby then said eagerly. "It's not more'n a few minutes down the road."

Leaving Parse to keep an eye on the hackney and their luggage, the Reddings and their cousin followed Mrs. Willoughby with varying degrees of enthusiasm. Constance looked doubtfully about her as they passed a millpond and several shops on the way to the village. "It is nothing like home," she complained.

Elisande had to agree. The village near their home in Sussex had been a friendly place with comfortable old trees and cheerfully thatched houses presiding over vegetable gardens. Camston-on-Sea was made of sterner stuff. The houses were constructed of rugged gray stone, and the trees had a gnarled and weathered appearance. Far in the distance they could hear the mutter of the sea.

"I am persuaded that I dislike that sound," Constance fretted. "I mislike the ocean—it is so wild and fierce."

"And *I* don't like the notion of living in a carpenter's cottage." Nigel's protest was spoken in a low tone so that Mrs. Willoughby could not hear. "This is a bacon-brained scheme, on my life."

Ignoring her family's doubts, Elisande asked the widow if the cottage had a garden. "Oh, yes, ma'am, that it 'as," exclaimed Mrs. Willoughby eagerly. "My man built two bedrooms off the big 'un—you'd call it a sitting room, I expect—and they both overlook t'back garden. Ever so sweet my roses are. I took slips from the old Norman Church, see."

Beside her, Elisande heard Nigel draw in a sharp breath. She looked questioningly up at him, and he said, "She's talking about an old church built near the sea. Used to ride there with—"

He broke off, his eyes shadowed with memory. Surely one reminiscence would spark another?

Elisande held her breath, but before Nigel could speak again, Mrs. Willoughby stopped in front of a cottage. " 'Ere it is," she announced.

Willoughby cottage was larger than the other houses. Set back from the road and screened by several willow trees, it also boasted a well-kept garden where rows of cucumbers and beans stood between marigolds, bright-eyed daisies, and phlox.

"Do you not think it is too small?" Constance whispered to Elisande. "There's not enough room for the three of us and Parse."

"Collect that we are taking the cottage for only a short time," Elisande whispered back. "I'm sure that it will be more comfortable than staying at the inn."

Nigel shrugged and turned away. Constance forbore further comment. "We should like to stay here on a weekly basis," Elisande told the widow. "If you will tell us the terms, Mrs. Willoughby—"

"The cottage ain't to let to the likes of you."

A small boy of about seven or eight was standing a short distance away. He was dressed in dusty clothes that seemed too big for him, and a battered hat had been jammed down on his head. A small, hairy gray dog of nondescript breed stood panting at his feet.

"Who is that horrid little boy?" Constance demanded as the dog began to bark.

"It ain't a boy—it's me daughter, 'Arriet," Mrs. Willoughby replied in a harassed voice. "Pay 'er no mind, ma'am—she ain't right in the 'ead."

"I'm not weak in the noddle, Mam," retorted the urchin hotly. "*You* are. If you think I'll let you rent our 'ouse to a traitor what sold our dad to the Frenchys—"

" 'Arriet," screeched her mother, "go away or I'll take a stick to you."

The child stuck out her tongue, whistled to her

dog, and darted off. "I do not think we are wanted here," Constance muttered.

"Don't pay 'er no mind, ma'am." Mrs. Willoughby 'was almost in tears as she explained. " 'Arriet's allus been a strange one. She was 'er dad's pet, seeing as 'e never 'ad a son, and 'e laughed at the way she dressed and all. Now that Sam's gone, I can't do nofink with 'er."

She turned to Nigel adding, "I 'ope you'll forgive me daughter's wicked tongue, sir. I never believed any of the gossip about you. Sam allus said as Mr. Parse was a honest man that wouldn't be in service to no traitor."

"I'm obliged for your good opinion," Nigel said dryly. "However, I'm not sure that it'll serve any purpose to stay here. We might as well—"

"I *cannot* believe it!"

The new voice was husky with shock. Nigel whipped around and gasped, "On my life—it's *you!*"

A young woman driving a perch-phaeton had come to a halt beside the cottage. Her huge green eyes were blazing with excitement, her red lips quivered with emotion. One look at the tempestuous face under the blaze of red-gold hair, and Elisande knew that this was Colonel Hanard's daughter.

Whispering her name as if it were a prayer, Nigel ran toward her. Next moment he had jumped back to dodge the whip blow Miss Hanard aimed at him.

"Stay away from me!" Sylvia Hanard shouted. "Beast! Coxcomb! How could you treat me so?"

Nigel had gone so white that he looked as if he might faint. Elisande ran to her brother's side and put a steadying hand on his arm.

"Nigel," she said angrily, "this lady wishes to have nothing more to do with you. I bid you good day, ma'am."

She glared at Miss Hanard, who completely ignored her. "Not one letter, not one word all this time," she said in a trembling voice. "You treated me as if I were no better than a—a serving wench. And I *waited* for you. I believed in you—"

"You *what?*"

Shaking himself loose of his sister's grip, Nigel strode forward and seized the horse's reins. "You waited for me?"

Miss Hanard's eyes flashed emerald fire. She raised her whip. Nigel did not budge. "Sylvia," he said sternly, "don't trifle with me. Answer me truthfully. Did you mean what you said? Do you still care for me?"

"Let *go* my reins, sirrah!"

Miss Hanard whipped her horses forward. Nigel let go the reins as the beasts sprang forward, and the perch-phaeton lurched away.

For a second there was deathly silence. Then Constance sneezed dispiritedly and plucked at Elisande's sleeve. "Are we still going to stay here in this dreadful place?"

Looking about her, Elisande saw that they had attracted a small audience. Women were leaning out of their cottages to stare, as was Mrs. Willoughby herself, and the big-eyed village urchins had gathered to watch the fun. A farmer on the way to market had stopped his cart to enjoy the drama.

"Can't we go back to Sussex?" Constance was pleading. "Look at poor Nigel. I'm persuaded it will be cruel to make him stop here."

Elisande hesitated. Perhaps Con was right. At the hands of such a vixen as Miss Hanard, Nigel's nightmares would probably grow worse, not better.

"Nigel?" she queried uncertainly. "Shall we go home?"

He was still staring after the rapidly vanishing perch-phaeton, and she had to repeat the question before he turned to look at her. "What? No, of course we can't go home."

Nigel began to stride down the road in the direction of the Gilded Stag. "Oh, where are you going?" Constance wailed.

"To find Parse and that damned hackney," he flung over his shoulder. "Didn't you hear her? Miss Hanard never got my letters. I have to find out *why*."

Short of chasing him down the street, there was little Elisande could do to stop her brother. She therefore went inside the cottage and inspected a tiny sitting room warmed by a large stone fireplace, a more or less adequate kitchen, and two minute bedrooms.

One of the bedrooms had a loft built above it. "This can be Nigel's room," Elisande decided, "and Parse can sleep in the loft. You and I will share the other room, Con."

"I'd be glad to cook and do for you, if you was willing," Mrs. Willoughby interjected hopefully. "My Sam said as I was a fair cook."

Hiring a cook would cost money that Elisande did not have. She courteously declined the offer and asked for Mrs. Willoughby's terms. The widow was a surprisingly shrewd bargainer, but Elisande haggled so adroitly as to drive down the price and earn Constance's astonished respect.

"I am persuaded that you made as hard a bargain as Parse ever did," she said as Mrs. Willoughby, promising to send for her belongings and those of Harriet, left them in possession of the cottage. Then she added in a relieved tone, "Here is Parse now—and Nigel, too, in the trap. I was afraid that he might follow Miss Hanard at once. But what has happened to your coat, Nigel?"

The young man was in a stamping bad temper.

24

"Some brats threw mudballs at us," he fumed as he strode through the door. "The widow's daughter led the mob." He spread his arms. "Look at me! I can't go to Hanard House looking like *this*."

"Nay, Captain, no need to be mithered. I'll have that mud brushed out right away," Parse soothed.

And, meanwhile, time would pass and Nigel would have time to calm himself. Elisande suggested that Constance lie down and hinted that Nigel should also rest, but he would have none of it.

More agitated than ever, he feverishly paced the length of the little sitting room. "How can she say that I abandoned her?" he muttered. "Would have died for her. She *knows* I would have died for her."

Elisande tried to sound reasonable. "No doubt it was just anger talking."

"Why should *she* be angry? She's the one marrying someone else, not me." Nigel fetched up at the room's one small window and stared gloomily down the village road. "Oh, Lord, why does she have to be so beautiful?"

Parse entered at this moment with Nigel's cleaned coat. Nigel shrugged it on and announced jerkily, "I'm going up to Hanard House now."

"So am I." Elisande met her brother's frown steadily. "Did you think I would let you walk alone into the lion's den?"

"It's not necessary that you come. Won't be pleasant at Hanard House." As his sister reached for her cloak, Nigel's voice rose. "On my life, Lisa, I don't *want* you to come."

As he spoke, Constance came out of the bedroom. She had put on her bonnet and was buttoning her traveling coat. "Don't tell me *you're* coming, too," Nigel exploded.

Looking pale but determined, Constance walked toward the door. "It seems I must."

"Why *must* you?" With an effort, Nigel lowered his voice. "Know you're both doing this for my sake—grateful, I assure you! But it's my problem, don't you see? I wish you'd stop home."

As if Nigel had not spoken, Constance went on, "I thought it wisest to consult the cards. When the Hierophant came up next to the Justice card, I knew that I must also go to Hanard House."

She walked out of the cottage and to the hackney. Elisande followed. Muttering under his breath, Nigel also took his place in the rented conveyance. "Hope you won't regret this," he growled.

Elisande hoped so, too. No one had much to say as the conveyance rattled through the village and onto the open road, and some ten minutes passed in silence before they came to a fork in the road.

"Where does the right road lead?" Elisande wondered as Nigel ordered the hackney driver to drive to the left.

"Toward the Norman Church and Swan's Cove." At her brother's terse reply Elisande felt suddenly chilled. Swan's Cove was where Nigel had been found that terrible night.

She glanced at him and saw that he had gone very pale and his eyes had an almost feverish glow. "How far to Hanard House?" she asked.

"As soon as we pass these woods, you'll see it above us."

Almost as he spoke, the hackney turned a sharp curve in the road, and Elisande swallowed nervously at her first glimpse of the colonel's home. As formidable as a fortress, the large stone house had been built on the crest of a hill and from thence seemed to menace the countryside.

Elisande recalled a letter she had received from Nigel shortly after his first visit to the colonel's house. "It's a great, grand, gloomy place," he had written. "Hanard House was built in the days of the Tudors, and they were always worried about enemies creeping up on them. Hanard House is built to repulse all invaders—on high bluffs with woods on three sides. On the fourth side, the house is protected by cliffs that look down over the sea."

Elisande could hear the sound of the waves as they rode up the slope toward the house. "How wild the sea sounds," Constance sighed. "Is not Miss Hanard afraid of it?"

"Sylvia isn't afraid of anything," Nigel replied proudly. "On my first visit here, she took me down steps cut into the cliff wall, and we walked down the beach to Swan's Cove. The sea was wild with the waves smashing against the rocks—you'd have hated it, Con! But Sylvia told me that she'd often sailed in such weather."

He broke off as they reached the top of the hill and rattled into a large courtyard. "Damnation," Nigel swore.

It was apparent that they were not the Hanards' only visitors. Several carriages, a phaeton, and three curricles stood in the well-appointed courtyard. Grooms ran to take the horses' heads, but Parse jumped down to do the honors himself.

"Happen t'captain'll need to have in a hurry," he told Elisande out of the corner of his mouth. "I'll keep t'hackney ready."

With this grim assurance ringing in her ears, Elisande followed Nigel, who was already striding up the wide stone stairs that led to the house. But while Constance exclaimed at the grandeur of the colonel's dwelling, Elisande only felt its menace. She strove to reassure herself that she had been right in bringing Nigel here. If any house held secrets, it was surely Hanard House.

Wooden-faced footmen in silver-and-blue livery opened the heavy front doors and requested to know whom they should announce. Since "Redding" would hardly be a welcome name, Elisande proclaimed in her most authoritative voice that Miss Constance Dayton and her cousins had come to call.

As they followed the footman up the stairs, muted sounds of music could be heard, and a woman's silvery voice called, "Lud! Now fortune *must* smile on me!"

On the heels of those words, the footman threw open a door. "Heavens," Constance breathed. "It is a card party."

In the high-vaulted, dark-paneled room— doubtless this had been the great room in Tudor days—tables had been set up. Ladies and gentlemen, resplendent in evening dress, were seated around those tables. The strains of an orchestra, playing on a raised dais under the oriel windows, were interspersed with laughter, exclamations of triumph or dismay, and the rattle of dice.

"It is a gaming party." Constance's small eyes roved anxiously from table to table as she continued, "My late papa used to go to many such—that is, before he went into dun territory and lost his fortune." Her voice faltered, and she added, "Elisande, this is not the time for Nigel to talk to Miss Hanard. Let us go away at once before we are discovered."

In spite of Constance's forboding, no one paid the least bit of attention to the newcomers. The gamblers were all intent on their game, and those who were not playing lounged about talking, flirting, or eating and drinking the offerings that servants carried about on silver trays.

Meanwhile, Nigel's eyes were sweeping the room as though it were a battlefield. "Where *is* she?" he muttered.

"Perhaps Miss Hanard is not here. I do not see her anywhere—"

Elisande checked herself as her gaze fell on a table that had been set up directly under a large oil portrait of King Henry VIII. There were several people sitting at this table including a broad-shouldered gentleman in evening clothes. The gentleman's elegantly arranged fair hair and intricate, snow white cravat cont·asted sharply with his deeply sunburned, hard-featured face.

She had not thought to see Lord Raven here. But, Elisande reasoned, since his lordship's brother was marrying Miss Hanard, it was logical that they would both be guests at Hanard House. She tried to continue her search for the colonel's daughter, but her eyes kept returning to Lord Raven. Apparently he liked gaming no better than he had enjoyed a visit to Lady Carme, for he was playing cards with barely disguised ennui.

"Elisande!" Constance was plucking at her arm. "That person with the fearsome mustaches is glaring at us."

A formidable individual in full regimentals was advancing upon them. Elisande's heart sank for, like his daughter, Colonel Hanard was unmistakable. His gray hair had been cut militarily short, he held himself sternly erect, and his steely gray eyes were those of a man used to unquestioning obedience.

"Nigel," Elisande hissed.

Her brother turned, saw who was bearing down on them, and instinctively drew himself to attention. His hand moved as if to salute before he caught himself. "Colonel Hanard," he began, "I must speak to you, sir—"

"You'll leave my house at once." In spite of his low voice, the colonel was quivering with fury. "How dare you set foot here after all you have done? Eh? Haven't you any sense of shame?"

Nigel flushed crimson but resolutely stood his

ground. "I came to speak to Miss Hanard," he replied. "Have a question for you, too, sir. Why were my letters to Miss Hanard never delivered?"

"You have the barefaced gall to ask me *why*?"

The contempt on Colonel Hanard's face was worse than a slap in the face. Elisande saw her brother's flush bleed away leaving him paper white as the colonel continued, "Whatever the board of inquiry decided, you are a despicable traitor, Redding. Eh? I could call you other names, but I restrain myself because we are in the presence of ladies."

Nigel's eyes narrowed. As Elisande put a restraining hand on his arm, she saw Lord Raven glance toward them. There was no mistaking the flicker of recognition in his lordship's bored blue eyes, and Elisande was mortified. Once more Lord Raven was about to witness the Reddings' humiliation.

But suddenly, there was a diversion. "Lud, I am spent," a lilting voice called. "Lord Raven, I believe you are in league with the devil to entrap a poor woman. I'm in dun territory unless I can get my husband to frank me."

A tall, fair-haired lady in a dress of black-figured lace over blue taffeta rose gracefully to her feet. "Cuthbert," she called merrily, "I beg you will redeem my vowels before I am dishonored. Lord Raven, I call upon you as a gentleman to allow me my revenge. We must sit down to cards again soon."

"I look forward to it eagerly," Lord Raven said in a voice that sounded anything but eager. He bowed to the lady in the black lace but kept his eyes pinned on Elisande. *What are you doing here?* those blue eyes demanded.

"You'll leave immediately, Redding. Eh? Either that or I'll have you thrown bodily out."

As the colonel snapped this command, the lady in black lace exclaimed. "*Surely* that cannot be Captain Redding?"

Nigel bowed. "Lady Graymount," he said. "Your most obedient servant, ma'am."

He was still deathly white, but he summoned a brittle smile as the lady glided toward him. "I have not seen you for so long—near a year and a half, if I remember," she exclaimed. "Won't you present me to these ladies with you, Captain Redding?"

Elisande was aware of Colonel Hanard's silent fury as Nigel's wooden voice made introductions. Her knees were shaking as she curtsied to the lady Nigel introduced as Lady Graymount.

"No—Mrs. Hanard," the blond lady corrected. "The dear colonel and I were married several months ago."

She smiled at the colonel who said peremptorily, "These people are leaving, Anabelle. Eh? Immediately."

"Not before I see Miss Hanard," Nigel persisted.

"Who wants to see me?"

Sylvia Hanard had swept into the room. Her glorious red hair had been arranged in a crown on the top of her head and was decorated with pearls and diamonds. Her dress of ivory satin banded with gold made her appear regal.

"She looks like a queen," Constance murmured in awe. "But who is that beside her?"

Trundling along at Miss Hanard's side trotted a small, round, middle-aged gentleman dressed in a plum-colored coat and matching breeches, a brocaded waistcoat covered with flowers, and white silk stockings embroidered with golden clocks. He should have looked like a buck of the first stare, but his carefully arranged brown curls, his intricate cravat, his quizzing glass, and his ornate gold-topped cane only served to make him look faintly comical.

"Ah, Lord Tanner," the colonel wife exclaimed, "I am much vexed with you. You were to have sat down at piquet with me, and instead you have been dancing attendance on my stepdaughter."

She stepped forward, slipped a hand into the stocky little gentleman's arm, and walked him away from the group. Meanwhile, Sylvia continued to advance, her eyes fixed on Nigel.

"*Why* are you here?" she cried dramatically.

"Sylvia," Colonel Hanard ordered, "leave this room at once. Eh? You may not speak to this man."

Ignoring her father, Sylvia spoke to Nigel in tones that throbbed with feeling. "Why have you come? I told you this afternoon what I thought of you."

"Eh? Eh? You have been skulking about, have you, speaking with my daughter behind my back?" the colonel roared. "Sirrah, the door. Thomas! Aylward! Escort this *person* out at once."

The laughter and talk died away, the musicians hushed their instruments. In the midst of almost utter silence, Nigel protested, "On my life, I did write to you. My letters were never delivered to you because your father kept them back. Ask my sister—ask my cousin if I didn't write to you every day."

Sylvia's huge green eyes turned to Elisande for the first time. "He's telling the truth," she acknowledged.

"He never stopped thinking of you," Constance added, then faltered silent when the colonel glared at her.

Her beautiful face ablaze, Sylvia Hanard wheeled on her father. "You told me that he had abandoned me. You *lied*, Papa!"

"Oh, I *say*," Elisande heard the marquess exclaim. He, like everyone else, was staring at their host and his daughter. Or, almost everyone. Elisande was conscious of Lord Raven sitting back in his chair, one solidly muscled arm thrown over the chair back. His bored look was gone, his dark face registered interest, but he kept his eyes squarely on Elisande.

Doubtless he was enjoying this Cheltenham tragedy. Elisande shook her brother's arm. "Nigel," she implored, "we must leave *now*."

Her brother paid her no attention. "How could you possibly believe that I was trifling with you?" he demanded. "Syl—Miss Hanard, I'm devoted to you. Give my life for you."

"I say—doin' it too brown, that," the Marquess Tanner protested. Swinging his walking cane, he advanced upon Nigel. "Young man, I'll have you know I'm Miss Hanard's affianced husband. Goin' to be married this comin' week. Festivities goin' on, and all that. Maybe you *didn't* know, so I'm tellin' you now. Sentiments of eternal devotion made to another man's affianced wife—deuced rackety thing to do. Mean to say, not *done*."

"I will *never* listen to you again," Sylvia informed her father. "You talk about honor until you are blue in the face and then you lie to me."

She held out her hands to Nigel. "And I will never marry anyone else," she promised. "Never, never, never!"

As her voice rose with each "never," the drawing room erupted into noise. The colonel began to bellow at his daughter, who screamed defiance back at him. The marquess said, "Oh, I say," several times, but kept his distance. Young gentlemen grinned; older ladies looked scandalized. Their lords appeared cynical. Young ladies whispered furiously behind their fans. The orchestra leader waved frantically, commanding his musicians to play, and the strains of a feverishly giddy country dance filled the air.

Up until now Lord Raven had been sitting and watching the commotion with great interest. Now he rose to his feet, strolled over to the colonel's side, and said, "A word, if I may."

He had to repeat himself twice before the colonel heard him. "What do *you* want?" Hanard barked.

"What you want yourself—an end to this regrettable scene," Lord Raven replied calmly. "My brother's a patient man, Colonel, but he doesn't want scandal involving his betrothed."

The colonel rolled a bloodshot eye at the portly, perspiring marquess and then back·to the marquess's younger brother. The horrible thought crossed his mind that Tanner was about to back out of the marriage.

"You're right, Lord Raven—eh? This is disgraceful," he spluttered.

"Look to your daughter, sir, and let me handle the rest," Lord Raven directed. Then, without waiting for the colonel's compliance, he turned to Elisande. "Ladies, I am Ivo Raven, your most obedient servant. Will you permit me to escort you away from all this?"

Elisande cast a distracted look at Nigel as Lord Raven slid one hand under Constance's elbow, the other under hers. "Leave me be," she protested. "I want to say here."

"You must be joking," Lord Raven said. "No one in her right mind would want to remain *here*."

"But Nigel needs—"

"Needs you to explain his actions? To apologize? Never apologize, Miss Redding, and never explain. Besides," he added as he began to stroll forward through the room, "military men are used to danger. They thrive on it."

Casting a despairing look over her shoulder,

Elisande saw that Mrs. Hanard was gliding toward Nigel. "Are you leaving so soon, Captain Redding?" she called merrily. "Will you not walk out with me?"

Without waiting for the young man's reply, she grasped him by the arm and almost dragged him along with her.

"You see?" Lord Raven went on calmly. He smiled at a sour-faced dowager in a puce turban, and frowned slightly at a young man who was staring at them through his quizzing glass. The dowager looked the other way, and the young man hastily dropped his glass. "Did your brother force you to accompany him here?"

"Of course not! My cousin and I insisted we come with him."

Elisande's words were lost in the colonel's bellows. "How dare you defy my orders? Eh? Go to your room at once."

Turning her head, Elisande saw that Sylvia Hanard was stalking across the room. As haughty as a lioness, she swept by the colonel's staring guests until she came to Nigel and Mrs. Hanard.

"At once!" roared the colonel.

Sylvia stopped a few feet away from Nigel, placed a white-gloved hand on her ruby lips and tossed the kiss to him. A sigh, punctuated by a protesting, "Oh, I *say*," from the small marquess followed her as, without looking at anyone else, she walked out of the room.

"Bravo," Lord Raven murmured. "That was worthy of Astley's Amphitheater."

Remembering that it was his lordship's brother who was Sylvia's fiancé, Elisande forgave him his sardonic tone. "Ah," Lord Raven added as they stepped out into the hall and began to descend the stairs to the ground floor, "here comes the hero of the piece."

Grateful beyond words, Elisande watched Mrs. Hanard lead the still bemused Nigel safely down the stairs. "No," she was saying firmly, "you must not go after her now, Captain Redding. Your sister is sure to agree with me."

Mutely Elisande nodded. If Mrs. Hanard had not removed Nigel as she had done, the colonel might have delivered an insult that no gentleman could have left unchallenged. Nigel in a duel—she shivered suddenly, and Lord Raven looked down at her curiously.

"I told you," Constance said suddenly. "I *told* you the cards foretold disaster."

Mrs. Hanard overheard. Raising her delicate eyebrows, she laughed ruefully. "Cards are fickle, as I know to my sorrow." Then she added, "I am sorry, Captain Redding. This has not been a happy night for you."

"It would have been worse, but for you," Elisande declared. "How can we thank you, ma'am?"

The colonel's lady gave Elisande a thoughtful look. "There is no need to thank me. I love my husband and I, too, didn't want to see him fight a duel. Besides, I know Captain Redding of old. I would not have wanted harm to come to him."

Elisande could think of nothing to say except, "Thank you for your kindness."

"And thank you, too, my lord," Constance said gruffly to Lord Raven. She looked down at the tips of her scuffed shoes as she went on, "Thank you for coming to the rescue."

Lord Raven bowed and suggested, "It might be wise to cut short this conversation."

From behind them came the sound of the colonel's bellows. Elisande grasped her brother's arm and urged him down the stairs toward the waiting hackney. He went as though he were walking in his sleep.

"Did you hear her say she never stopped loving me?" he asked her. "The colonel kept my letters from her. Don't blame him—if I had a daughter I wouldn't let her within ten feet of an accused traitor—"

He broke off and began to gnaw his knuckles. "Let us go home," Elisande sighed.

She felt exhausted and dispirited. Far from helping Nigel, their visit to Hanard House had made things worse.

Chapter Three

Standing by the window of a private coffee room at the Gilded Stag, Lord Raven watched gray clouds boil across the horizon. A storm had rolled in late last night and had raged till dawn, but the worst of it was over and now the bad weather was in retreat before a westerly wind.

"Sailing weather," his lordship muttered.

Last night he had dreamed of a fresh gale, rain squalls, and a heavy sea running. The dream had been so vivid that he had awakened disoriented in his stuffy room at the inn. Perhaps it was the changeable weather that made him feel at once so bored and so restless, Lord Raven thought, but his irritation was more likely caused by Wigram's latest start.

Why should his brother, after forty-five years of assiduously avoiding parson's mousetrap, fall madly in love with a spoiled redheaded chit at least twenty years his junior? Raven could make neither head nor tail of it. "But she'll lead him a devil of a dance," he mused. "Poor old Wigram."

A gust of wind hurled pellets of rain against the window, and Lord Raven cursed softly. He would have given anything to feel that audacious wind in his face and the deck of the *Silver Raven* beneath his feet as it sailed eastward before the westerlies.

"Disgustin' weather!" The Marquess Tanner came squishing into the coffee room, shaking himself free of water as he came. Raindrops slid off his curly beaver, down the seven capes of his greatcoat, and puddled around his sopping boots. "Rainin' pitchforks and shovels still."

He broke off to sneeze. "I say, I've caught a deuced cold," he added plaintively. "Weather in these parts deucedly unhealthy."

"May lord."

Gliding regally into the room, a tall, slender individual proceeded to divest the marquess of his dripping outer gear. He cast a blighting look at the marquess's ruined hat, murmured through his narrow nose that he would commence to pour a footbath for his lordship in his suite, and advised that a cup of chocolate taken in front of a roaring fire would be the thing against inclement weather.

The marquess pulled a face. "Chocolate—that's deuced paltry stuff, Landers. Brandy'd do the trick better."

"Spirits, may lord, are not what Dr. Stuyshollow suggests," the valet responded coldly. "We must take heed against the gout. If you will warm yourself, I will bring the chocolate."

Lord Raven raised his eyebrows as the haughty valet glided out of the room. "Your man takes good care of you," he commented.

His elder brother nodded rather gloomily. "I'd be lost without him, Ivo. Trouble is, he knows it. Deuced superior sort of chap, is what I say. Makes me wonder who's the master and who the servant, sometimes. It's most provokin'."

He walked up to the cheerful fire burning on the hearth and stirred it with the tip of his wet boot. "Landers's hipped because I rode out to Hanard House this mornin' in the rain," he sighed. "It was wasted effort, anyway. *She* wouldn't see me."

"You knew that before you went," Lord Raven pointed out. "Face it, Wigram. You didn't have a prayer the moment Young Lochinvar came riding out of the west."

"Young Lo—oh, you mean, Redding." The marquess attempted to harden his round, good-humored countenance into a scowl. "What I say is that the man's nothin' but a deuced scoundrel."

"Give it up, Wigram."

"Shan't," the marquess retorted. "This is all a passin' fancy. Miss Hanard's a female, and females are doocedly fanciful and romantic. It's their nature. She'll come around to her senses when the madness and moonshine wear off."

"Quoth the colonel," observed Lord Raven cynically. "Hanard'll say anything. He's afraid you'll cry off."

The marquess preened himself. "The colonel's a good man. Mean to say—took an instant likin' to me."

"More likely he took to your warm pockets," Lord Raven pointed out, but his brother only looked mulish.

"Nothin' wrong in that. Money makes the world go 'round, and all of that. I say, Hanard'll see to it that the girl does her duty. The marriage *will* take place."

Though sorely tempted to shake some sense into his bird-witted brother, Lord Raven restrained himself. Experience told him that it would not help. Good-natured though he was, Wigram could be extremely stubborn when crossed, and once an idea had wormed itself into his thick head, it stayed there until such time as the marquess himself cast it aside.

"So you've decided to stay on and woo the fair Sylvia." The marquess nodded defiantly. "Good. I'm leaving for Scotland in the morning."

An expression of extreme alarm filled the marquess's round eyes. "I say," he gasped, "not doin' a bunk on me, Ivo?"

Coldly Lord Raven pointed out that he was not about to hang about Dorset forever. "I came with you because there was to be a wedding. Since it's been canceled, I need to be about my affairs. The repairs on the *Silver Raven* will have been completed by now, so I'm off to Calais."

He was interrupted by a cry of distress as the marquess bowled across the room and seized his younger brother's arm. "Oh, I say, Ivo," he bleated, "you wouldn't desert a chap now. Not like you, not like you at all. I need you, old fellow. Need you desperately."

Landers chose this moment to glide back into the coffee room. He carried a salver on which reposed a cup of steaming liquid, a glass of water, and several pills in a silver dish. "Your medicinals, may lord," he intoned.

"Hang my deuced medicine," shouted the beleaguered marquess. "Take the deuced things away instanter!" The valet stood his ground and fixed his employer with a frigid eye. "I told you I don't want 'em," the marquess continued, but in a much smaller voice. "I don't need anythin' that deuced quack gives me."

"If we do not take these pills, may lord," Landers announced, "our gout will return, our head will commence to ache, and we will undoubtedly contract the grippe."

The marquess seized the pills, downed them in a gulp, and fell to coughing violently. "Happy, are you now, Landers?" he gasped as his brother pounded him on the back. "Nearly scragged me."

Unimpressed, the valet murmured that the footbath had been prepared, likewise a mustard plaster in case it was required. He bowed and exited.

"Damn the man," the marquess choked. "To perdition with him and his mustard plasters. Ivo, you don't mean to say you're runnin' off to sea again, are you? I mean to say, old fellow, you've got deuced good agents all around the world, ain't you? Let *them* carry on your business for you."

Another fit of coughing seized him. Somewhat alarmed, Lord Raven pounded his brother's back again, and after a while the marquess wheezed, "What do you want to go to Calais for? You've stopped your junketin' around the world, ain't you? You promised the mater that you'd stay in Scotland. Don't you remember that? Told her you and I would watch out for each other."

Lord Raven sighed and said he had not forgotten. "But I'm leaving Dorset tomorrow," he added.

"Ivo, if you're going to leave me here alone, my goose is pissed."

Wigram was almost in tears. "She means so much to you?" Lord Raven wondered.

"Sylvia Hanard is my life and my soul," quoth the marquess feelingly. "*Help* me, Ivo."

Swinging away from his brother, Lord Raven returned to the window. "Shall I help you, Wigram?" he mused. "Shall I?"

"Oh, I say, old fellow, that's what I've been askin' you to do."

"And will you do what I tell you to?"

"Anythin'. Climb a mountain, if I have to. Swim a blasted river. Or—I would, that is, if I could swim. Mean to say—I'll do anythin'!"

Anxiously the marquess watched his younger brother's reaction to this stirring speech. Ivo had always been the clever one in the family, the adventurer who traveled all over the world and made a fortune, the handsome one, the one who cut his stick at nothing. Humbly and without a shred of envy, the marquess recalled that Ivo had the golden touch and succeeded at whatever he did whereas he, Wigram, usually made a muck of things.

Ivo was always right—except in the matter of the beautiful Miss Hanard. Without the love of Sylvia Hanard, the marquess knew, his soul would wither and wilt and his life would be an endless desert of regret.

"I say—will you help me, old fellow?" he repeated anxiously. But it was all right. Ivo was turning back from the window, and he was smiling kindly.

"Go and have your footbath," he was saying. "Landers has been waiting for a good fifteen minutes."

"But what'll you *do*, Ivo?"

"I'm going to pay a call on Captain Redding," he said. "My man says they've taken lodgings in the village."

"Call on—I say, Ivo, I don't know as I like the sound of that. Unless you're goin' to offer the plaguey traitor your cartel?"

Patiently Lord Raven explained that far from challenging Nigel Redding to a duel, he was going to set about gaining the young man's confidence. "If he sees that I don't mean him harm, he'll be more likely to listen to me," he added.

The marquess seized eagerly on this. "And then you can tell the deuced bounder to lope off!"

"On the contrary, I'm going to encourage him to stay." As his brother stared, Lord Raven explained, "Your Sylvia thinks Nigel Redding is a romantic figure because he's lost his memory."

"I *know* all that! The question is, I say, what's to be deuced done about it?"

"I'll tell Redding that you, as a fair and decent man, have suggested a truce between you. Neither of you will interfere with the other."

Lord Raven put an arm around his brother's chubby shoulders. "And when next you visit

Hanard House, you'll tell Colonel Hanard that, sensitive as you are to his daughter's feelings, you're willing to give her time to make up her own mind."

The marquess pulled free of his brother and shouted, "I deuced well won't do it, Ivo. Make up her mind, forsooth! Why, she's bound to choose that—that—"

"That's why we're going to help Redding regain his memory."

The marquess stopped stuttering and looked thoroughly bewildered. "I don't understand," he sighed.

"You don't have to."

"But look, Ivo, I think Redding never lost his memory at all. He'll never admit to bein' a traitor, and so Miss Hanard'll never stop feelin' a *tendre* for him. Where will that leave me?"

But Lord Raven only smiled and said to leave it in his hands. "Females like your Sylvia thrive on drama," he explained. "Let matters settle down and she'll lose interest in Redding. Think of it, man—he's as poor as a church mouse and disgrace haunts his name. But if the two of you remain at drawn daggers, she'll never choose the right man."

The marquess considered this. "The right man, you say? Well, well. You've got the brains in the family," he said at last. "I don't pretend to understand but—I know *you* know, and that's what counts." He began to leave the room then paused to add feelingly, "I say, Ivo, you're the best brother a man could ever have. Helpin' me like this, I mean."

Lord Raven's smile turned wry as he watched his brother trot out of the room. "The question is," he murmured, "will you thank me for my help in the end?"

"Is it still raining, Lisa?"

Pausing by the small window, Elisande peered

skyward. "Perhaps the sky is getting a little lighter," she said.

"That is what Nigel said," Constance began, then broke off to sip tea from a cup at her elbow. "I warned him that it was foolhardy to go out walking on such a day, but he would not listen. I am persuaded that he means to walk toward Hanard House."

Elisande watched her cousin drinking tea and wished that Constance's skill with herbs could brew up something that would clear Nigel's head. Since that disastrous scene at Hanard House three nights since, Nigel had been beside himself. The lost look he had so often worn in Sussex had been replaced by a feverish determination to see Miss Hanard.

"She never got my letters. Doesn't know what's in my heart. Have to tell her somehow," was what he had said that morning.

Finally losing patience, Elisande had demanded, "And how do you propose to tell her? The colonel has forbidden you the house, and Miss Hanard has been forbidden to leave it. Besides, what good will any of this do when she is to marry the Marquess Tanner?"

But Nigel would not give an inch. "She swore she wouldn't marry him or anyone else. Lisa, don't you remember how she threw me that kiss? Felt it burn me like fire. On my soul," he had added passionately, "I *must* find some way to see her."

Then he had announced that he was going for a long walk. "If he walks up to Hanard House and tries to see Miss Hanard," Constance was saying now, "that fierce colonel may shoot him. Cannot you reason with him?"

"I've tried." Elisande shook her head in frustration. "You know as well as I do that Nigel will listen to no one when he is in one of these moods.

Short of hiding his clothes and boots, there is nothing any of us *can* do."

Through the thin wall, they could hear Nigel readying himself for his walk. "Miss Hanard is a great beauty," Constance said wistfully. "I am persuaded that *she* never sat on the fringe of parties with the old ladies when the dancing began. No doubt gentlemen always fell over themselves to ask her to stand up to them."

She was interrupted by a sudden bellow. "Goddamn that wretched beast to everlasting hell," Nigel roared.

Elisande gasped and Constance started up as Nigel came striding into the little sitting room. He wore one boot and carried its mate in his hand.

"Where is that bloody brat? I'll wring her neck. Where *is* she?"

"Where is who—and what's wrong with your boot?"

"Harriet Willoughby's damned dog has chewed a hole in the toe," bellowed Nigel. "Look at it!"

If it had not been so serious it would have been comical, Elisande thought as Nigel waved the boot almost under her nose. Meanwhile, Parse was trying to explain why it could not have been his fault that the captain's left boot had been savaged.

Just then there was a yapping bark outside. "There's the little beast," Nigel snarled.

Drawing on his ruined boot, he stormed through the door. Parse followed. Elisande and Constance ran to the doorway and saw Harriet walking some distance from the house. As usual, Alexander trotted at her heels. When she saw Nigel, she stuck out her tongue and darted off.

With a muffled oath, Nigel dashed off in pursuit. "Oh, this will never do," Constance wailed.

As she spoke Alexander came panting back down the road and ducked behind the house. "This way,

Captain! Us got t'bugger now," Parse shouted to Nigel.

The two men disappeared around the house. There was a yelp, a string of curses followed by a thud—and then Alexander came pelting out and made off down the road.

Elisande ran down the wet steps and to the side of the cottage where she found Nigel sitting in a puddle of mud. Before she could say anything, a deep voice called, "Good morning to all."

Elisande jerked her head around and saw Lord Raven. He had halted his curricle near the cottage and was watching the proceedings with interest. "I seem to have come in a moment of crisis," he commented. "Is there something I can do?"

In spite of his helpful tone, Elisande saw that his lordship's lips were twitching at the corners. She cordially wished him in Jericho. Once again he had come just in time to observe the Reddings at their worst.

"Nothing needs to be done," she informed him coldly. "My brother slipped and fell, that is all."

"Fell while I was chasing that bloody dog." Too furious to be embarrassed, Nigel got to his feet. "Brute chewed a hole in my boot," he fumed.

Hoots of derisive laughter interrupted him. Lord Raven followed the direction of Nigel's glare and saw that a gaggle of village boys was standing down the road. In their midst pranced a small, gray mongrel. "If I ever catch that beast within ten yards of me," Nigel threatened, "I'll drown him."

"You touch Halexander, an' you'll be sorry" was the shrill retort. "You're nothing but a coward and a traitor, too. Traitor, traitor, trai-tor!"

As the urchins darted off, Lord Raven watched the fight go out of Nigel Redding. The young man looked as if he were facing a firing squad, but the look in his sister's eyes was even more pitiful.

Elisande walked over to Nigel and put a hand on his arm. "Let it go, dear," she said gently. "What has happened can't be helped, and boots can be mended."

But at the same time she was wondering, *how*? She could tell that Alexander's teeth had done irreparable damage. The boot would have to be replaced—and that would cost money that they did not have.

Nigel seemed to read her thoughts. "Can't afford new boots," he growled. "Besides, there probably isn't a decent bootmaker in these godforsaken parts."

"Yes, there is." Nigel jerked his head around at the sound of that deep voice. So did Elisande. In their misery, they had totally forgotten about Lord Raven.

"There's a bootmaker some miles away past Allford," Lord Raven went on. "I know that because Hanard mentioned that he'd had some excellent footgear made locally. I'll be glad to convey you there, Redding, if that's your inclination."

Nigel started to speak, then looked down at himself and became aware of his muddied condition. His voice was stiff with mortification as he replied, "Kind of you, Lord Raven, but I couldn't impose on your time."

Lord Raven ignored the hurt pride in the younger man's voice. "Nonsense," he said pleasantly. "I'm going that way myself and would enjoy the company."

He smiled in such friendly fashion that Nigel felt the wind taken out of his sails. "Thank you again, my lord, but I won't keep you." Then, as Lord Raven did not budge he added even more uncertainly, "Are you driving on to Allford now, or will you—"

"Or will I stay and have some refreshment? Now,

I call that kind." Lord Raven promptly dismounted, handed the reins to his waiting groom, and strolled forward adding, "Count yourself fortunate that you are in a civilized country where there are such things as bootmakers. I was not so fortunate. While in the Sandwich islands, I lost *my* footgear to a ferocious wild boar."

"I am afraid that there is nothing but tea in the house," Elisande protested.

"There's nothing like a good cup of tea."

Raven looked hard at Miss Elisande Redding and perceived from the slight flush over her high cheekbones and the look in her eyes that she was embarrassed and unhappy that he had come. Such large eyes she had, and the shadow of her dark lashes brought to mind a lake he had once seen in the New World. Half-hidden amongst the trees, it had had the clearest water he had ever seen with shadows and flickers of sunshine glimmering gold at its heart.

With some effort Raven reminded himself that he was visiting the Reddings for Wigram's sake. "I would be glad of a hot cup of tea," he repeated. "Unless I intrude?"

Mindful of the laws of hospitality, Nigel assured Lord Raven that he was not intruding in the least. Constance scurried into the cottage to prepare more tea, and Elisande followed with foreboding.

She was sure that Lord Raven had come to warn Nigel never again to see the marquess's fiancée and, no matter how diplomatically such a warning might be put, she could imagine Nigel's reaction to it. Elisande racked her brain for some way to soften the blow that was sure to come but could find no ready answer. She could only stand by mutely as Nigel sent Parse out for more wood and Constance offered Lord Raven the best chair in the tiny sitting room.

"You must drink the tea hot after riding in such weather," Constance said in her gruff little voice.

"I enjoy the wind and drizzle," Lord Raven replied. "It's fine sailing weather and reminds me of the sea." He took the proffered cup, sipped, and looked mildly surprised. "This is excellent tea—very unusual."

While Constance flushed with pleasure and muttered something about brewing rose blossoms and spearmint with exactly the right kind of honey, Elisande strove to think of some safe topic of conversation.

"I collect that you said you had 'just returned' to Scotland, my lord," she said at last. "Were you away from England?"

Emboldened by the compliment to her tea, Constance ventured to add, "In some foreign country, perhaps?"

Raven smiled at the small, brown lady. "Have you visited other countries, Miss Dayton?"

"I prefer books about herbs and bees," Constance said gruffly. "It is Elisande who loves tales about faraway countries and yearns for adventure."

"I am only an armchair traveler," Elisande protested, but Raven noted that there was a wistful note in her voice. "My late father and I took many an imaginary expedition together. No doubt you have actually journeyed much farther than I have ever dreamed, my lord."

"I have gone up the coast of America," Lord Raven said, "and from there through the Baltic Sea to Saint Petersburg. Down, then, to stops at Cape Town and Île-de-France and finally to Canton, China."

Elisande's gasp interrupted him. "Have you truly been in China? Perhaps you have even visited the Forbidden City?"

She held her breath until he shook his head.

"I've only gone as far as Whampoa, on the Pearl River. From there I rode on a sampan to Canton. Unfortunately, the Forbidden City is closed to all."

Nigel was looking interested in spite of himself. "You mentioned America," he prompted.

"Boston was my first port of call. A rough voyage—the Atlantic is an angry ocean in the winter."

Lord Raven's descriptions of that journey were so vivid that Elisande could actually imagine herself sailing into a tempest. She could almost feel the icy sea spray on her face and the wind whipping through her hair. Finally, enthralled, she shared Lord Raven's excitement at seeing the New World at last.

"The New World. Now that's a place that suits me to the ground," Nigel mused. "A place where a man can start out fresh. Start clean."

"Quite so," Lord Raven said quietly.

In the silence that followed, Elisande's fears returned with a vengeance. Now, she thought, Lord Raven would tell them why he had come to see them.

But instead of doing so he asked for more of Constance's tea. "If your recipe isn't a secret, I'd like to ask it for my brother," he said. "The poor fellow has a cold in the head. Not surprising since he insisted on riding to Hanard House in the worst of the rain."

Nigel spoke abruptly. "Forgive me, Lord Raven, but I'm not one to wrap plain facts in clean linen. Have you come here on your brother's business?"

"In a manner of speaking," Lord Raven replied, and Elisande's heart bumped painfully. Supposing Lord Raven had come to goad Nigel into fighting a duel?

"My brother is an honorable man," Lord Raven was saying. "He respects Miss Hanard's feelings and understands your problem. So, until you regain your memory, my brother suggests a truce. Neither of you will interfere with the other or take action against the other while the truce lasts."

"A truce until I regain my memory?" Nigel turned away bitterly. "Tanner may have a long wait, my lord."

"Have you tried to see Miss Hanard?" Lord Raven asked. "I only mean," he added mildly as Nigel jerked around to face him, "that talking to her might bring back the past."

"I've tried to see her." A flush stained Nigel's lean cheeks as he admitted jerkily, "Not easy. She's been locked into her room by the colonel. On my life, I only want to talk to her. Know well that I have nothing to offer her."

He broke off, turned on his heel, and stalked wordlessly to his room. "Lord Raven has not had his second cup of tea," Elisande said in a low tone. "Con, I will help you brew another pot."

But as she was about to follow her cousin into the kitchen, Lord Raven said, "Don't look so worried."

Elisande stopped short. "I beg your pardon?"

"I said, don't worry. Your brother will think it over and decide that a truce makes sense. And the bootmaker *is* reasonable and won't press for payment."

"You are being very kind to us." Resolutely Elisande met his eyes and asked, "Why? There must be a reason."

Lord Raven nodded as if to say, of course there is. "Wigram is a good fellow, Miss Redding," he explained. "He enjoys planting fruit trees and growing strawberries and likes to potter about his estate at Tanner. Do you think such a life would suit Sylvia Hanard?"

Elisande thought of the beautiful and dramatic Sylvia and remained silent.

"I couldn't wait to shake the dust of home from my boots. Wigram, on the other hand, is like Anteus and cannot stand to be far from his estate. His latest project is to start an apiary and enjoy his own honey." Lord Raven's smile was both affectionate and impatient. "Wigram would like to consider himself a huntsman, but he is so tenderhearted he can't bear to kill a living creature. Once I found him in tears because he had found a rabbit in a trap."

"And, of course, *you* do not weep over rabbits," Elisande could not help murmuring.

"I don't believe in weeping at all. There's no help in tears—and no need for them. Far better to recognize change as inevitable and enjoy each new experience as it unfolds."

With more than a trace of envy, Elisande thought that Lord Raven looked like a man who lived each moment to its fullest, and the devil take the hindermost. For a moment she wondered how it must feel to be a rich gentleman who could indulge his every whim and travel to the most exciting corners of the earth. Then she stifled an involuntary sigh and asked, "Why are you telling me this?"

Without answering the question, Lord Raven asked one of his own, "Your brother really doesn't remember what happened on that night, does he?" She shook her head. "Poor devil—that must be pure hell."

The unfeigned sympathy in his lordship's voice was as disconcerting as it was unexpected. Elisande had armed herself to protect and defend, and now found herself at a loss as Lord Raven went on, "When I was up at Oxford, I was in a hunt accident that left me with so many broken bones the sawbones wasn't sure I'd ever walk again. I had to lie without moving so much as a muscle for three months—lie there, not knowing if I was going to be a cripple."

He paused and looked down into her face. "Believe me, that experience made me realize how perilous life is and how precious, too. What happened to me is much the same that happened to Redding—only the paralysis is in his mind."

Constance had returned with a fresh pot of tea and had been listening silently. "That is why Elisande said that we must come to Dorset," she now interposed. "She hoped that Nigel would remember once he came here. But so far, things have been going from bad to worse."

"Perhaps we can help each other," Lord Raven said. "Wigram and Miss Hanard will never suit, but my brother is a stubborn man. He feels that the girl will eventually come to her senses and marry him—which she won't do, of course. As far as she's concerned, a more interesting suitor has presented himself."

Constance looked shocked, but Elisande was relieved by Lord Raven's plain speech. So this was why he had come—not only to deliver a word of truce but to encourage Nigel to pay his addresses to Miss Hanard!

Only, this would never do. "I am not sure that Nigel should court Miss Hanard either," she said frankly. "Doing so in the face of her father's objections may hurt my brother more than it helps him."

"Not if it jolts his memory."

Lord Raven lowered his tone. "I once sailed with a man whose head was well near cracked open during a storm. When he came to, he didn't even remember his own name. It took another furious tempest to bring his memories back."

Constance clasped her stubby hands. "It makes sense, Elisande. 'The hair of the dog that bit you,' as Papa used to say. Only, I fear Papa was speaking more of brandy than of memory."

With his eyes on Elisande's worried face, Lord Raven added, "Gentle treatment is useless in this case, Miss Redding. Bold measures are called for, and by working together we can pull it off. Then Wigram will go back home to his bees and fruit trees, and a dark cloud will be lifted from your brother's life."

The words caressed her mind tantalizingly. Elisande thought of Nigel, not as he was now but whole and safe and well again, full of eagerness and vitality.

"It is too wonderful for words," she whispered.

The change in her face caught him by surprise. Like the sun bursting through dark clouds at the eye of a storm, Elisande Redding's eyes glowed with unexpected hope and joy. It was the unexpectedness of it that caused Lord Raven's heart to jolt almost painfully—and before she could say more, Nigel entered the room.

Lord Raven greeted the young man with something akin to relief. "Ah, Redding," he exclaimed. "Ready to go to the bootmaker, are you? No, really, I intend to carry you off."

"If you're certain I don't impose—" But Lord Raven brushed such protests aside. He picked up hat and gloves, bowed to the ladies, and ushered Nigel out of the door.

When they had gone, Elisande went to the little window and watched Lord Raven and her brother walk away to the waiting curricle. *Together we can pull it off,* he had said.

"Do you think Lord Raven really means to help Nigel?" Constance asked.

"As long as it suits his purpose." But this, Elisande knew, was only a very temporary arrangement. She had no illusions. Once the marquess had come to his senses and gone home to his estate, Lord Raven would have no further use for the Reddings. And if during the course of events it suited Lord Raven to abandon Nigel, he would do so without a second thought.

"Lord Raven is a fascinating man and tells such wonderful stories," Constance mused from her place near the fire. "He can be most charming."

From the window Elisande watched the way Nigel was admiring Lord Raven's matched grays. There was an eagerness in his stance that she had not seen in a long time. "Yes," she murmured, "so he can."

There was a short pause, and then Constance sighed. "This makes no sense."

No, life made no sense at all. Anxiously Elisande watched his lordship's curricle ferry her brother away until Constance said, "Look at this."

Elisande turned to see Constance sitting at the table by the fire. She had pushed the tea things away and had spread out her tarot cards.

"I thought that in a case like this we should consult the cards," Constance explained. "They have a way of seeing what we do not." She tapped one of the cards. "See, here is the Knight of Pentacles, which represents a fair-haired person: Lord Raven. The cards say that his lordship is intelligent, resourceful, fearless, determined—and—"

"And what, Con?" Elisande wondered, as her cousin paused to frown at her spread of cards.

"The cards are contradictory. They suggest that as fascinating as he is, Lord Raven is also an opportunist who can be devious—even deceitful." Constance broke off and added anxiously, "Elisande, even though Lord Raven *is* our ally, I—I don't believe that we should trust him *too* much."

Chapter Four

"You sound cheerful this morning," Elisande commented. "Are you driving out with Lord Raven?"

When Nigel nodded, morning sunlight turned his fair hair to silver. "Going driving near the Norman Church where I used to ride with Syl—where I used to ride. Raven thinks that might jog this damnable memory of mine."

For once he seemed almost cheerful about it, and in spite of her ambivalent feelings toward that gentleman, Elisande had to admit that Lord Raven had accomplished a minor miracle.

Scarcely a day had gone by during the past week without some visit from his lordship, who would arrive at Willoughby Cottage on his curricle and drive off with Nigel. By degrees Nigel had lost that brittle, haunted look and actually seemed hopeful that matters would turn out well. He had put on a little weight, his color was good, and Parse had reported joyfully that there had been not even the ghost of a nightmare.

"Where did you drive yesterday?" Constance was asking. "You were gone for several hours."

"We drove down to Swan's Cove where they found me that night. Should have remembered—but there wasn't even a flicker." Nigel paused to add, "On the way back, we met Sir John Fowles—he lives not far from here—and he asked us to go along and look over some horses that were going under the hammer. You never saw such handsome animals, Lisa. Raven thought so, too—bought four perfect goers."

Then Sir John had invited Lord Raven and his companion to sample some punch at the Silver Dragon. As Nigel reached for another piece of toast, Elisande's gratitude increased. Without Lord Raven's patronage, Sir John might well have given the former Captain Redding the cut direct.

"It'll be a fine day for a ride," Nigel continued. Constance drew a deep breath that was not quite a sigh, and he actually grinned. "Don't tell me that your cards have been croaking again, Con?"

"I was thinking of the marquess," Constance explained. "It must be hard for him to see you become bosom bows with his brother."

Nigel's eyes hardened at the thought of his rival. "Wouldn't waste sympathy on Tanner," he snorted. "Truce or no truce, I'll wager the fellow's hoping to find a way to discredit me. Don't trust him, on my life."

"But you trust his brother, Lord Raven," Elisande pointed out.

"Raven's a man of the world. He knows that nothing will be settled until I remember what happened that night."

As Nigel stretched out his long legs, Elisande recalled that she had still more to thank Lord Raven for. Not only had the bootmaker been extremely skillful, but his bill had been next to nothing.

"Horses—that's Raven now," Nigel exclaimed. He caught up his riding coat, kissed his hand to the ladies, and went whistling to the door.

"I never thought to hear him whistle again," Constance said happily. "Your plan is working, Elisande!"

Leaving Elisande clearing the breakfast table,

she bustled off into the bedroom from whence she could be heard singing off-key as she made up the beds. Blended with those unmusical notes, Elisande could hear Lord Raven's deep voice outside, and then Nigel's exclamation of surprise and pleasure. A moment later, she heard his brisk footsteps at the door.

Without turning her head, she said, "There's much to be done here, so I will not come out to greet Lord Raven. Make my excuses for me."

"Your excuses are not accepted."

Elisande nearly dropped the breakfast plates as she saw Lord Raven standing in the doorway. He was dressed for riding in a fawn-colored riding coat that perfectly fit his broad-shouldered frame and breeches that delineated the hard muscles of his thighs. "Good morning, Miss Redding," he said. "And, for once it is a very *good* morning, more like late summer than autumn. The sun is golden and the blackbirds are singing in the hedges."

His deep voice filled the stuffy little cottage with bright images, and Elisande suddenly recalled a time when she and Mama and Papa and Nigel had gone riding together in the Sussex woods. They had taken a picnic basket and Papa had read to them about the magical continent of Africa.

It had been autumn then, too, but an autumn gone long since. Aloud Elisande said, "It sounds magnificent indeed, and I wish you and my brother a fine drive."

She accepted to carry the dishes into the kitchen but Lord Raven strode purposefully across the room and took them from her. "At least come outside and approve the horses I brought for our excursion. From what your brother tells me about your prowess as a rider, you'll prefer the mettlesome gelding. Miss Dayton will no doubt be grateful for the mare."

"What gelding, what mare?" Elisande interrupted, completely bewildered. "What are you talking about, my lord?"

"Come and see," Lord Raven said.

Elisande walked to the door, then stood staring. Four horses stood in front of the cottage. Nigel, oblivious to the rest of the world, was running his hands over the flanks of a dappled gray gelding, while a coal black stallion tossed its head nearby. Two other horses, one a gentle-eyed bay mare and the other a handsome young chestnut gelding, cropped at the clover.

Involuntarily she took several steps forward, and as if it sensed Elisande's presence, the chestnut tossed its fine head and whickered softly. Her heart contracted in sudden longing. On such a horse she could ride as free as the wind.

There was an exclamation behind her. "Oh, heavens," Constance said faintly, "such enormous, fearsome beasts!"

Elisande turned to see her cousin in the doorway. "Don't worry, ma'am," Lord Raven was soothing. "The man from whom I bought these horses swore his youngest daughter rode that mare. You'll be as safe as a church on her."

He looked, Elisande noted, pleased—no, *smug*. He looked as though he were sure of her reaction and compliance.

"I collect that this is your way of inviting us to ride," she said coolly. "It is very kind of you, but my cousin and I are busy."

"Oh, on my life, Lisa," Nigel protested, "doing it too brown, aren't you? Can't be so busy as to want to stay stuffed into that damnable cottage all day." He broke off to add eagerly, "Chestnut's a beauty, isn't she? She's the pick of the lot that went under the hammer yesterday. And, Con—the mare's so gentle even you would like her. On my life, you will."

While Constance swore that she could never like anything so *large*, Lord Raven walked up to Elisande's side. "Besides hoping for the pleasure of your company, I have another reason for asking you to ride with us," he said.

When he smiled, his eyes changed to the color of a summer sky and his hard face softened into a most persuasive eagerness. Elisande could imagine the effect of that charming smile on female hearts and distrusted it profoundly.

"We are going to ride toward the Norman Church today. From what he's told me, this is a place where Nigel and Miss Hanard used to ride together." So it was *Nigel* now, Elisande noted. "Something might touch his memory, but I might not see it. You know him better than any living soul. *You* would know."

"But surely Nigel himself would know if anything came back," she argued.

"It might only be a flicker of memory— something too small to really notice." Lord Raven nodded toward Nigel, who was coaxing Constance to pat the gentle mare's nose. "When we're together, I sometimes get the feeling that Nigel's on the brink of remembering. It's at that moment when you could help him. The right word from you might help him breach the wall."

It sounded reasonable. Perhaps there had already been missed opportunities, moments when she could have helped Nigel through the shadows of his clouded mind. Elisande caught her breath at that thought and said, "Give me a moment to change."

Looking pale but determined, Constance announced that she, too, would ride out. "I feel that I must," she told Elisande as they went into the cottage to change. "I laid out the cards this morning before breakfast, and they informed me that something *unexpected* was going to happen. And then, I drew the Hierophant *and* the Justice card. I am persuaded that my presence is necessary if Nigel is to recover his memory."

It did not take long for the ladies to dress in their riding habits. Elisande's leaf green costume had been much used in its time and fit her like a time-tried old friend, but Constance's navy blue habit smelled strongly of camphor and had apparently never been worn.

"I put it on once," she confessed as they approached the horses. "That was the day I rode with Papa in the park."

"Really, Con? I always thought you could not abide horses."

Constance flushed crimson. "My horse stopped to graze on dandelions, and when I tried to move it, it threw me over its head."

"Oh, poor Con," Elisande exclaimed. "Were you hurt?"

"Only my dignity. Everyone stared so." Constance went on sadly, "and Papa lost his temper and shouted that I was a disgrace to the family and had no bottom. It was a disaster."

She approached her mare with nervousness bordering on panic, but Lord Raven himself held the reins for her and assured her of the animal's gentle nature. "I'm glad you came with us, Miss Dayton," he added seriously. "I have been wanting to ask you a question about your tea. I gave the recipe to my brother's valet, but it's my opinion that the fool left out one of the ingredients."

"Possibly he used the wrong honey." Constance exclaimed. She plunged into a discussion of bees and hives, and became so involved that she scarcely noticed when Nigel handed her up.

Here was yet more evidence of Lord Raven's charm, Elisande thought. But though she was on her guard with this gentleman, she was grateful to him for having persuaded her to ride out. It was a beautiful autumn day, the sun was warm on her face, and the sounds of blackbird and thrush were sweet in her ear. Late summer flowers bloomed along the wayside, and trees glowed with fall colors.

"You look as if you're dreaming," Lord Raven said, pulling in beside her. "Or are you remembering?"

"Both," she admitted.

"Autumn has its charms," Lord Raven allowed. "In the tropics there is little difference between seasons. I'm told that Englishmen who live there many years miss spring and autumn most."

"How many years were you abroad?" she wondered.

"Nine years in all," was the prompt answer. "I left as soon as I was finished at Oxford. No one was surprised since I was the second son, but to be honest I'd have gone away even if I were in line for the title. England is too tame for me."

So he had taken passage to Boston and from thence to the port of Salem. "In Salem I bought a clipper ship which had once been used as a privateer. Such a sweet, wild, swift devil—but perhaps I am boring you?"

Elisande realized that she had been hanging on his lordship's words. "I have never been on a ship myself," she confessed, "but I have often wondered how it must feel to sail the ocean. When I was very young, I would lie awake at night pretending my bed was a ship in the middle of the sea."

"A calm sea?"

Too caught up in her own imaginings to care if Lord Raven was laughing at her, Elisande shook her head. "Not always. How it stormed in my imaginary ocean! There were heavy seas so that my ship sailed close under reefed main-top sails. Often I had to lash myself to the mast to be safe from mountainous waves."

"You're familiar with nautical terms, I see." Now there was real interest in his eyes.

"Papa was fascinated with ships and explorers, and he read us adventure stories when we were children. Nigel liked to hear about shipwrecks, but I preferred tales of faraway lands." Elisande smiled reminiscently. "I even made up one of my own—Farland—where people lived in tree houses made of gold."

Lord Raven chuckled, and Elisande checked herself. Why, she wondered, was she nattering on in this fashion? She had confided these adventurous daydreams to no one, not even to Nigel. She shot a swift look at Lord Raven and saw that he was listening intently.

"I've never visited a place like Farland," he admitted. "In fact, my first sea voyage on the *Ebony Raven* involved scudding up and down the American coast. I had to learn how to sail first, after all." She nodded. "I hired a crew—four officers and twenty-four before the mast, including me."

"You were a crew member on your own ship?" When he nodded, Elisande was astonished. What sort of aristocrat was Lord Raven?

He was saying, "I didn't stay a seaman for long, of course. I learned quickly and promoted myself to third mate on the second schooner I bought. While on the *Emerald Raven*, I learned to navigate."

"How many ships do you have?" she asked curiously.

"Two clippers, two square-riggers, a sloop, and my schooner. The *Silver Raven* is in Scotland now, but I plan to sail her to Calais when I return."

"How fortunate you are!"

Lord Raven smiled. "Fortune favors those who take risks."

And no doubt he had taken risks and enjoyed taking them. "Nine years of adventure—and you never missed England," Elisande mused.

"Would you?" Lord Raven asked and saw her turn to glance back at Nigel and Constance, who were riding some distance behind them.

"Perhaps not, but I would miss the people I love," she replied quietly.

Faraway, magical places dissolved and coalesced into a winding English road bordered by thickets of English oak and ash. "You came back, too," Elisande pointed out.

"After my father's death. Mother was not well either." A shadow touched Raven's strong features as he added, "I thought it was time to leave my business ventures to my managers in Salem, Bombay, and Calais, and settle down in Scotland near Tanner Place where Wigram lives."

The unfeigned warmth in his voice nudged awake a corresponding emotion within her. No matter what he said, Elisande knew that Lord Raven, too, had returned home to someone he loved.

She nodded her understanding, and they rode together in companionable silence. Odd, Raven thought, that silence could be so easy between them. Of the many women he had known, most had wanted to flirt, to talk, to be entertained. Others had been so restless they had never been happy except when dancing, or hunting, or gambling—which was the way of young Mrs. Hanard. The colonel's lady would lead Hanard into dun territory if he did not take care, but the man obviously doted on his charming young wife.

"His rose without a thorn," Raven murmured.

"You are thinking out loud." Elisande regarded him with sympathy as she added, "I do so often when I am worrying about Nigel."

Before Raven could respond to this, three riders—two riding together and one following at some distance—cantered around a bend in the road. Even at this distance, Elisande recognized the lead riders as Marquess Tanner and Miss Hanard.

"Good Lord," Lord Raven exclaimed. "I underestimated Wigram. I wonder how he managed to coax Miss Hanard to come riding with him?"

Elisande turned in her saddle to see if Nigel had caught sight of the oncoming riders. She was in time to see her brother jab his spurs into his gelding's sides. Disregarding Constance's cries of protest, he galloped away.

Truce or no truce, it would be awkward if they met. Elisande started to ride forward, but Lord Raven caught her reins. "What are you doing?" she cried indignantly. "Let go of my bridle immediately!"

"Let the lovers meet, first," Lord Raven said so calmly that her eyes narrowed in sudden comprehension.

"You planned this. You *knew* that those two were riding this way."

Instead of answering, Lord Raven trotted his horse forward, drawing Elisande with him to where Constance was sitting her horse uneasily. "I suppose this is what the cards meant when they said, that something 'unexpected' was going to happen," Constance said in a worried voice.

The lovers had met in the center of the meadow some distance away. Nigel and Miss Hanard were deep in conversation, and the marquess was endeavoring to edge his horse between them without much success.

"I say—this ain't done," they could hear him bleating. "The truce, remember? You're not supposed to interfere with me, Redding, and if this ain't deuced interferin' I don't know what is. Deuced smoky thing to do, that's what I say."

"What are you going to do?" his lordship asked, as Elisande once more urged her horse forward.

His tone was one of mild interest. "I am going to try and prevent a confrontation," Elisande said, through her teeth. "It will not help Nigel if the marquess loses his temper and challenges him to a duel."

"Wigram?" Lord Raven repeated in amazement. Then he threw back his head and roared with laughter. "Wigram fight a duel—oh, my lord."

Elisande set spurs to her mount. It was her fault, she thought bitterly, for letting down her guard. Lord Raven was nothing more than an irresponsible opportunist who had doubtless engineered this meeting to see what would happen if Nigel and Sylvia Hanard met unexpectedly. He had brought two volatile people together without thought of the consequences.

Elisande called out to Nigel, but neither her brother nor his lady paid any attention. They did not appear to know that anyone else besides themselves existed in the world.

Suddenly Miss Hanard snapped a command to her groom, touched her horse with her spurs, and shot away. Nigel immediately followed. The marquess yelped, "Oh, I say—come back!"

He set spurs to his own mount, which bounded forward in pursuit of the lovers. "He won't be able to keep it up for long," Lord Raven observed.

Almost as he spoke, the marquess's horse stopped abruptly. Elisande cried out as the marquess himself shot over the horse's head and thudded to the ground.

"Wigram has the worst seat in England," Lord Raven commented, philosophically. "He hates horses as a rule—but love does strange things to a man."

"And I thought you cared for your brother," Elisande exclaimed.

Without waiting for an answer, she rode forward. But by the time she had reached his side, the marquess had sat up and was gazing after the rapidly dwindling figures.

"Are you injured, Wigram?" Lord Raven asked. "Haven't broken anything, old fellow?"

The marquess's brown wig had fallen off revealing scanty salt-and-pepper tufts of hair. He rolled his eyes but made no sound except for a faint groan. "Oh, heavens, you *are* hurt," a new voice exclaimed.

Constance had also ridden up and was scrambling out of the saddle. "Don't move, I beg you," she cried. "People who suffer falls should not *move*."

The marquess looked with vague surprise at the small, flushed female who was bending over him. Then the rigorous training of a lifetime asserted himself, and he struggled in vain to get to his feet.

"Servant, ma'am," he mumbled. "Caught me in a deuced awkward moment. Beg you'll excuse me for not risin'."

"Pay it no mind at all," Constance replied. Too agitated to be shy she added, "You have sustained a bad fall and you have a nasty cut on your temple. Here—let me wrap my handkerchief about your forehead."

"It don't signify about my forehead." The marquess stared after the rapidly disappearing riders as he added, "I say, Ivo—she didn't even take her deuced groom. Why ain't you followin' them?"

"All in good time," Lord Raven said. "First tell

me how you convinced Miss Hanard to come riding with you."

An enormous sigh rumbled like an earthquake through the marquess's rotund frame. "Went to see her at Hanard House this mornin', same as I always do. I begged her to go ridin' out with me. Didn't think she'd come, Ivo—almost fainted when she agreed! The colonel was in raptures—I was in heaven. We thought that maybe Miss Hanard was comin' to her senses. But," he added sadly, "all the time she was plannin' to meet Redding. Deuced traitor's been poachin' on my preserves."

The sympathy that had been building up for the marquess received a sharp setback. Elisande glared at the stout man. "Nigel is no traitor!"

The marquess ignored her. "Don't sit there grinnin', Ivo," he pleaded. "Go after that fellow and call him to account."

"If the ladies will consent to wait here with you, I'll be off," Lord Raven agreed, but Elisande was already spurring her horse toward the now distant specks.

"*Did* you know that they would be riding out here?" she demanded as Lord Raven pulled alongside her.

"It was an educated guess." Lord Raven met Elisande's frown with an ironic smile. "Come, Miss Redding, isn't this what we hoped for?"

He spurred ahead of her, forcing her to gallop in order to keep up. "But how did Miss Hanard know Nigel was here?" Elisande shouted over the pounding of hooves.

He shrugged. "My groom met Miss Hanard's abigail in the village and *mentioned* that young Captain Redding sometimes drove out to the Norman Church. Naturally, the girl told her mistress."

Light blue eyes caught and held hers in a cool,

level look. "Life is full of chances, Miss Redding. And choices."

"This is not a game for us," she protested angrily.

"Nor for me. I assure you I'm sick of stopping in Dorset—one of the most incredibly boring places I have ever seen—and having to dine with Colonel Hanard and listen to Wigram's complaints. Don't hurry so much," he went on as Elisande spurred forward. "Let them be alone. Let them talk. Can you think of anything that would be more likely to jog his memory than a ride with Miss Hanard?"

"They are disappearing into that copse of pine trees," Elisande pointed out. "We may lose sight of them."

"My guess is that they will dismount as soon as they find a private place" was the cool reply. "They won't get far."

Elisande looked back over her shoulder to where Constance was helping the marquess to his feet. "Con's cards spoke true again," she muttered.

His smile turned sardonic. "Her tarot cards prophesied this meeting?"

"The cards warned us not to trust you, my lord."

"Very wise," was the prompt reply. "Never trust anyone unless your goals are the same. But since my brother's happiness is tied to Nigel's recovering his memory, there's no reason to distrust my motives."

They had reached the thicket of pines as he spoke, and Elisande had to bend to avoid low-hanging branches. It was very quiet here except for the trill of songbirds, and the branches grew together to form such a dense canopy that the sun's rays dappled only here and there. Amongst the dark evergreens, a few maples flamed with color, and a bright yellow butterfly fanned its wings against a bank of purple asters.

"We'll have to dismount and lead the horse to the

church," Lord Raven was saying. "Nigel showed me the spot where he and Miss Hanard held their trysts. I imagine they are there now."

He swung down from the stallion and reached up to help her. There was determination in that hard clasp, a confidence that Lord Raven would always get exactly what he wanted. As the strong hands clasped her waist and lifted her down, Elisande felt unaccountably unnerved.

"Don't worry so much," he said softly. "I want what you want."

Had he actually read her mind? Elisande's eyes flew up to meet his, and she caught her breath at the expression she saw there. "Do you?" she managed to say.

"Yes. Quite apart from wanting to get Wigram away from parson's mousetrap and myself out of Dorset, I believe your brother's innocent of the charges against him."

The words were so unexpected that they brought tears to her eyes. She tried to blink them away, but they lay caught in her thick, dark lashes. Like dew drops glistening on a flower, Lord Raven thought inconsequentially.

And then she smiled, and her smile was like summer sunshine. Raven felt a wave of desire wash over him, so strong and unexpected that it shook him to the bones. The world, the quiet woodland in which they stood, Wigram and all his concerns, all evaporated from his mind leaving nothing but the brilliance of one woman's smile.

The way he was looking at her made her feel— Elisande caught her breath. Confused, she took a step backward and fetched up against her gelding, who snorted his disapproval. Surprised, she reacted by stepping forward again—stepping into Lord Raven's arms.

The protest that was on her tongue trembled into

nothing as his mouth came down on hers. The woods disappeared. Nigel and Con and Miss Hanard vanished like puffs of smoke. Even the ground she stood on slid away. Elisande found her only reality in the hard arms that held her so closely and the passionate warmth of Lord Raven's lips. For the first time in her life she felt as if she were cut adrift in time and space, clear of any thought or emotion save for a sweet, soaring rush of exhilaration.

"Sylvia—as God is my judge, I love you."

At the sound of Nigel's desperate voice, reality returned like a thunderclap. For a moment she stood immobile. Then gasping her dismay, Elisande attempted to push herself clear of Lord Raven's arms.

"To say that I don't love you is like—like saying the sun isn't shining," she could hear Nigel protesting. "Naturally I love you. Love you to distraction."

"No, you don't," Miss Hanard wailed. "Not if you act this way."

What way was he acting? But his words made Elisande suddenly recall how *she* had been acting. Even worse, Lord Raven's arms were still clasped around her waist. "I beg you will release me instantly," she cried.

Lord Raven dropped his arms and took several steps backward. To say that he was astonished at his own behavior was putting it mildly. The idiotic impulse that had moved him to kiss Elisande Redding had disappeared leaving him wondering whether he had gone soft in the brain.

More likely, he had been too long in Dorset. Raven called himself unprintable names in three different languages as the unseen Sylvia mourned, "If you loved me as you say you do, you would do as I say. We could be over the border in two days—"

"No, I tell you," Nigel interrupted. Then he

added sternly, "On my life, Sylvia, I love you too much to do anything so—dishonorable. You'd be ruined. Think what that would mean."

There was a swish of skirts and, inching forward, Elisande could see Miss Hanard standing and facing her brother in the clearing. Her bonnet with its emerald plumes had been cast aside, her costly riding cloak hung open to show her magnificent figure. Her red hair glistened in the scanty sunshine, and her emerald eyes were bright with tears.

"What does my good name matter?" she cried. "I only want to be Mrs. Nigel Redding."

Nigel half turned away, and Elisande read despair on his face. "That's just *it*. Damn it, Sylvia—can't marry you and condemn you to life with a—with a suspected traitor."

"You a traitor? You are nothing of the kind, Nigel. You know it and I know it," Sylvia Hanard began.

"No," Nigel said bitterly. "I *don't* know it."

There was a little hush in the glade. Elisande's heart nearly stopped beating at the misery in her brother's voice. "I don't *know* what happened the night of March thirtieth," he was saying. "I remember the party. Remember seeing you—you looked so beautiful, Sylvia. Remember your father locking those dispatches in the safe."

He broke off and shook his head in despair. "After that, there's nothing. Blank as a wall. I try and try, but it's all gone. Next thing I know, I'm lying on the sand at Swan's Cove with that bloody dispatch from Wellington in my pocket."

"You are not a traitor," Miss Hanard protested. "You aren't! I believe in you."

"Your father thinks differently. Can't blame him. On my life, I think I'd believe it myself, in his shoes." Nigel rumpled his fair hair in his agitation. "Sometimes I even wish I knew that I was a traitor. At least, then I'd *know*. Driving me insane, Sylvia. Now, how can I ask the woman I love to share my nightmare?"

Sylvia Hanard flung herself forward into Nigel's arms. She wrapped her arms around the young man's neck and kissed him passionately.

Beside her, Elisande heard Lord Raven utter a word of approval. She herself was transfixed with horror. Not only were they shamelessly spying on an intimate and terrible moment but she herself had also been held in a man's arms like that, not three minutes ago. She herself had been kissed as Sylvia Hanard was being kissed. And the worst of it was that a part of her wanted to be kissed again.

No, she thought. *No!*

"No, I tell you!"

Nigel broke away from Sylvia Hanard's arms and staggered backward. There was a wild look in his eyes, and his cheeks were drained of every bit of color. "I won't do this," he grated. "I'd kill myself rather than hurt you, Sylvia. Can't you see why we mustn't elope?"

"If you loved me, you would," Sylvia Hanard retorted.

She began to cry in bitter earnest. Nigel slumped against a tree. Lord Raven cursed under his breath.

"He won't remember anything after all those dramatics. We might as well bring down the curtain on this Cheltenham tragedy."

There was a harsh disappointment in his voice that grated against Elisande's vastly bruised emotions. His lordship had no concern for Nigel or for anyone else. All he wanted was for the marquess to give up courting Miss Hanard so that he could leave Dorset.

And she had allowed such a man to kiss her. She was more shameless than Sylvia Hanard, Elisande thought miserably as she listened to Lord Raven crashing about the underbrush in order to alert the lovers to their arrival. At least Sylvia believed that she loved Nigel and wanted to marry him while she, Elisande, had no excuse at all.

Chapter Five

The ride homeward was a grim affair. Miss Hanard, who had once more commanded her groom to fall back, rode ahead and all alone, her head tossed high to show she did not care a whit for the fair-haired young man who rode close behind her.

"Regard the way that Nigel is chewing the inside of his cheek," Constance sighed to Elisande. "He reminds me of the fable of the Spartan boy and the fox."

Nigel looked perfectly wretched. He was very pale and clutched his reins as a drowning man might clasp at straws.

"I wish I had never suggested we come to Dorset," Elisande exclaimed. "I wish Lord Raven had never befriended him or taken us riding so that he could meet *her*."

She glanced sideways at Lord Raven, who was riding beside his elder brother. The wind carried away what was actually being said, but the marquess was talking a great deal and gesturing in an agitated manner. Lord Raven said nothing. His sun-dark profile could have been a cameo cut in stone.

In fact since leaving the woods he had not so much as glanced in her direction. "I am a bird-wit," Elisande muttered.

Misunderstanding, Constance reached out a small, gloved hand to comfort her cousin then hastily withdrew it to steady herself on her mare. "It is not your fault that Miss Hanard is a heartless minx."

Elisande recalled how the "heartless minx" had sobbed and sobbed and felt like weeping herself. She had come all the way to Dorset and used up almost all the money they had in the world, and it had not helped Nigel. All that had happened was that an adventuring lord had as good as given her a slip on the shoulder.

"The village idiot has more sense than I have," Elisande exclaimed.

"You only meant for the best." Constance paused to add gruffly, "I feel sorry for the marquess. He is so much in love with Miss Hanard, and she does not care a rush for him."

Lord Raven was riding too far from the Redding ladies to hear what they were saying, and if truth be told he did not want to know. He was disgusted with himself because even when he was not looking at her, he was extremely aware of everything Elisande did.

He kept his gaze fixed on Sylvia Hanard who was riding thirty yards ahead of them with her nose in the air. "Like a queen, a deuced queen," Wigram was sighing. With Constance's handkerchief wrapped about his head, he had a vaguely piratical look, but his eyes were full of woe. "Look at how she's sittin' her horse," he went on. "No female in England can touch her."

Lord Raven thought of Elisande Redding riding beside him and talking about her imaginary voyages. "Don't have anything more to do with women, Wigram," he said abruptly. "They bring nothing but trouble."

He had no idea what had made him kiss Elisande Redding. Worse, though he had no notion why, while he was kissing her he had totally forgotten the common sense and cool blood that had taken him unscathed through difficult spots all over the world.

Once, while riding across a sea of grass in the New World, one of his guides had actually been struck by lightning—and had survived! Now he knew how that man had felt. In the instant when Elisande's slender body had nestled against him, Raven had felt a jolt so powerful, so inexplicable, that it still shook him.

"Bloody hell," Lord Raven muttered.

Abruptly he spurred his horse forward, cutting off his brother in midlament. The marquess started to follow, then thought better of it and slowed his mount to fall in beside Elisande and Constance.

"I say, you must think me rag-mannered," he commenced awkwardly. "I mean to say—didn't even thank you, Miss Dayton, for your kindness when I, er—the mishap, you understand." Constance ducked her head and growled that it was nothing. "No, not nothin', deuced kind," the marquess persisted earnestly. "I must have bored you by natterin' on and on about Tanner Place."

Constance shook her head. "Not at all, sir. Your descriptions of your estate and the motherless little pigs were most interesting."

The marquess looked gratified, but before he could speak, a puff of wind caught Sylvia Hanard's handsome bonnet and carried it sailing across the heads of the party. Nigel immediately turned his horse and cantered off in pursuit. With an excited, "Oh, I say!" the marquess also sawed his horse around and followed the runaway hat.

Sylvia halted her mare and watched as her two suitors galloped madly after the bonnet, which swirled and dipped in the wind. "I say, bung off—this is my business," the marquess was heard to shout at Nigel. "Go away, Redding. Poachin' on my preserves—not ton at all."

"How ridiculous they are," Constance gruffed. "Like two boys chasing a hoop."

But the gentlemen on horseback were in deadly earnest. As Nigel outspurred his rival, Elisande saw the marquess raise his riding crop and aim an ineffectual blow in the direction of the other man's horse.

"They will hurt each other," she exclaimed. Turning to Lord Raven, who had drawn up his horse some distance away, she called, "Pray stop this foolishness."

"Not I," Lord Raven retorted. "Leave them alone. The exercise will cool them both down."

Just then the bonnet blew upward, frightening the marquess's horse. It whinnied, pawed the air, then wheeled around and began cantering off in the wrong direction.

"I can understand why he does not like horses," Constance commented worriedly as the marquess was carried off in spite of his curses and entreaties. "They are so large and unruly and cannot be trusted. There! Now Nigel has got Miss Hanard's hat."

Bending gracefully from the saddle, Nigel picked up the bonnet and carried it to his lady like a trophy of war. They were too far away to hear what he said as he handed the hat over, but Elisande saw the way her brother caught Miss Hanard's hand in his, bent, and kissed it passionately.

Sylvia Hanard snatched her hand away, spat out some word of rejection, and spurred her horse forward. Nigel started to follow, then drew back and watched her go.

Fortune was fickle, Raven thought cynically. He watched his brother careening down the field and pronounced himself completely out of patience with all these people and their problems. "Let them go to Hades for all I care," he muttered to himself. "And confusion take Wigram for keeping me in this cursed place."

The devil of it was that he was not free to leave—not yet. With barely concealed impatience Raven trotted his horse over to Nigel, who was breathing hard and staring after the vanishing Miss Hanard.

"I'd better follow Wigram and make sure he isn't hurt," he said abruptly. "I leave it to you to accompany the ladies back to the village."

With a valiant effort, Nigel managed to pull himself together. "No need to fear for the horses we're riding. I'll have my man bring them to you at the inn."

Beelzebub seize the horses, Lord Raven nearly shouted. Then he forced himself to review his plan of reawakening Nigel Redding's memory. It was a flawed plan at best, but it was also the only thing he could think of.

Forcing a smile he said, "No, don't do that. These horses need exercising on a regular basis. I'd be obliged to you and the ladies if you'd ride them whenever you can. Your man can stable them at the Gilded Stag in the meantime."

He cantered off, but Nigel stayed where he was until Elisande rode over to him. "It's time to go home," she told him gently.

"She'll have no part of me, Lisa. Despises me." Even now, Nigel could not tear his eyes away from Miss Hanard's disappearing back. "Can't blame her. Despise myself, on my life."

"Let's go back to the village" was all she could think to say. "Con will brew one of her strongest teas to revive us."

At least once in the cottage they could bar the door and lick their wounds in peace—but this was not to be. As Parse was leading the horses off to be stabled, an elegant barouche came bowling down the village street.

Constance knit her brows nearsightedly. "I collect that is Mrs. Hanard handling the ribbons."

There, perched above a pair of matched dapple-grays sat the colonel's wife. She looked elegant in an afternoon dress of pale blue jaconet muslin. Her riding cloak of the same color matched her blue kid gloves and the jaunty ostrich plume that curled down from her bonnet to cup her cheek.

Elisande watched the lady's arrival apprehensively, but Anabelle Hanard smiled as she called, "Good day, Miss Redding—and Miss Dayton, too. I didn't think to catch you at home on such a beautiful day."

Tossing her reins to her groom, she allowed Nigel to hand her down. "Have you been out riding, Captain Redding?" she asked then amended contritely, "Lud, I forget that I must call you 'Mister' now."

Muttering an excuse about seeing to the horses, Nigel bowed and walked hurriedly away after Parse. "I am sorry if I caused him pain," the colonel's lady exclaimed.

"It has been a difficult day," Elisande said. Then, because it was the only polite thing to do, she added, "Will you come inside, Mrs. Hanard?"

"With pleasure—only, you must call me 'Anabelle,' my dear—and I shall call you Elisande."

With a charming little nod and a flurry of skirts above neat blue boots of the finest leather, the colonel's wife ran up the stairs and into the parlor. "Lud, but this is divinely quaint," she exclaimed. "How clever it was of you to take these pleasant lodgings instead of stopping at that tiresome inn."

She tossed off her gloves, accepted the offer of a cup of tea, and ensconced herself in one of the better chairs. "Tell me, Miss Dayton, how go the cards for you these days?"

Constance, who was on her way to the kitchen to make the tea, looked somewhat at a loss, but apparently the colonel's wife did not require an answer. "I myself have had the most shocking run of bad luck lately," she sighed. "I thought to turn bad fortune into good by wagering my diamond earbobs last night, but I lost them to Sir Giles Moorhaven. Lud, can you credit that? You can imagine how the colonel glumped at me."

Elisande murmured something sympathetic. "Actually, it is cards that bring me here," the colonel's lady went on blithely. "I've come to carry you off, Elisande—and Miss Dayton, too, if she will come. There is to be a gathering to cards at Mrs. Dinrail's this afternoon. She is a most amusing woman and gives excellent gaming parties."

Constance declined the pleasure at once. More diplomatically, Elisande explained that they had no skill with games of chance. "It would be a case of throwing good money after bad, I'm afraid."

The colonel's wife laughed her silvery laugh. "Sensible women. I agree with you entirely, but— heigh-ho, this is the country and so *flat* that one could scream for sheer boredom." She paused to add with a touch of irony, "Gaming is the only entertainment in miles. One must do something to keep from being bored to death."

She paused a moment before adding, "This isn't the only reason I came. I meant what I said the other night, Elisande—I wish us to be friends. Now, I ask you as a friend—how is Mr. Redding?"

Elisande was trying to find words to frame a reply, but Constance forestalled her. "Until today he was much improved," she sighed. "But now that he saw Miss Hanard, there has been a setback."

"He met her by chance," Elisande made haste to explain. "She was riding with the marquess near the Norman Church."

A look of pure mischief filled Anabelle Hanard's expressive blue eyes. "Do you tell me so? My step-daughter did ride out with her intended this morning. Cuthbert was so delighted that Sylvia had softened toward the Marquess Farmer that he let his daughter ride off with only her old groom to attend her."

"'Farmer' is not his name," Constance pointed out.

"No, but it suits him. The man has actually nursed piglets. With his own hands, I do assure you!"

She went into peals of laughter. "But that was because the mother sow died," Constance explained earnestly. "The marquess did not want the little pigs to starve."

"Oh, tol rol," the colonel's lady said. The mischievous light in her blue eyes gave her the appearance of a naughty child as she added, "So he told you the story? The marquess has made a friend, I see."

Turning quite pink and mumbling that she would make the tea, Constance scurried out. As soon as she had gone, Anabelle became serious once again. "I take it that your brother's memory has not returned? Lud, my dear," she added as Elisande hesitated, "I'm no fool. I guessed at once that you had brought Mr. Redding here to try and jog his poor memory. It is what I would do for a brother—if I had a brother."

She sounded so sympathetic that Elisande felt a hard knot form in her throat. "My plan is a failure," she admitted. "Nothing Nigel has done has brought his memory back."

"But what *has* he done besides the meeting with Sylvia?" The colonel's wife drew her delicately arched eyebrows together. "I'm persuaded that you are going about this the wrong way, Elisande. I would say that the answer lies at Hanard House."

She leaned forward to speak most earnestly. "Except for that one night, Mr. Redding has not set foot in the house. He has not visited the garden, or the conservatory, or the colonel's study. These are the places most filled with helpful memories. These are the places he should go."

"The colonel has forbidden Nigel to set foot in Hanard House," Elisande pointed out. "It's not possible."

"Impossible while Cuthbert is at home, agreed. But," Anabelle added mischievously, "tomorrow evening, he will be away, and *I* invite what guests I choose."

She smiled meaningfully at Elisande, who exclaimed, "Are you sure it would be safe?"

Anabelle Hanard rolled her eyes. "Oh, lud, yes, my dear. Cuthbert is dining with General Hollingsdale who lives on the road to Allford and is undoubtedly the greatest bore in the county. The two of them will talk about military exploits till all hours."

Once more she grew serious. "Don't think that I am betraying my husband's trust, Elisande. I'd not do that for the world. But I remember how much Cuthbert liked—and, I am persuaded, still likes—Captain Redding. Having the captain's innocence proven would make the colonel very happy." She paused. "*I* believe your brother is innocent. It is a shame that so many others do not."

Lord Raven does. The thought came unbidden to her mind, but she ignored it. Lord Raven, Elisande reminded herself, was not concerned with Nigel's innocence or guilt. He had other fish to fry.

Anabelle Hanard was urging, "Bring your brother with you to the house tomorrow about nine. Sylvia and I are invited out to dine with Lady Aylmer, but I will make some excuse and remain at home. We will have the house to ourselves."

Elisande nodded eagerly. "Parse can watch the road to make sure we are not interrupted," she said.

"Good. I will make sure that there are no servants about to carry tales." Anabelle paused. "Perhaps it were best not to tell Miss Dayton about what is to happen. The fewer who know about it, the better."

Constance returned at this point with the tea. After sampling a cup and proclaiming it interesting and aromatic, the colonel's wife rose to take her leave. Chattering merrily about her card parties and gaming losses, she tripped down the stairs to her waiting barouche.

Constance eyed her doubtfully. "I am persuaded that Mrs. Hanard is a rattle who thinks of nothing but gaming," she commented.

"It was kind of her to call," Elisande hedged. She felt a little guilty not telling her cousin about Anabelle Hanard's plan, but that lady's warning made sense. Con would probably want to come along and, since she feared the dark even more than she feared horses, she might well spoil everything.

Elisande did not even tell Nigel until that evening. She coaxed him to walk with her in the garden after supper and then explained what Anabelle had proposed. "What is the last thing you remember about that night?" she asked.

He knitted his brows in an effort to concentrate. "Remember being out in the garden looking for Colonel Hanard. That's all."

Nigel shook his head in frustration, and Elisande took his arm. "I, too, believe that the answers are waiting at Hanard House. Perhaps it will all come back tomorrow."

Next day, Nigel was a bundle of nerves. He ate nothing at breakfast, was curt to Constance when she worried about his lack of appetite, and later snapped at Mrs. Willoughby, who had come to collect the rent.

"Can't you control your daughter's mongrel?" he flared. "The brute snapped at my heels when I went riding this morning. If he destroys anything more of mine, I'll drown him."

Mrs. Willoughby burst into tears and called heaven and earth to witness that a widow's life was a hard one. " 'Arriet just needs someone to talk to 'er, firm like," she sobbed. "It isn't easy to raise a child without a man in the 'ouse."

Suddenly, she turned to Parse. "Per'aps you could 'ave a word with the child, Mr. Parse? She looks up to you so much, an' all."

"Me!" exclaimed the horrified Yorkshireman. "Nay, that's gormless. I know naught about children."

"But you 'ave such patience, Mr. Parse, and you're such a big, strong man and all. 'Arriet and me, we look up to you so," the widow pleaded. "Just a word with 'er, now—it'll work wonders, I'm sure, and she won't never bother Mr. Redding no more."

Nigel uttered an exclamation of impatience and strode off, and Parse looked after him worriedly. "T'captain's in one of his black moods," he told Elisande when the two of them were alone. "Miss Lisa, it puts me in mind of t'times before a battle. Happen summat's mithered him sore—summat that I don't know about?"

The last had been twisted into a question. Swearing Parse to secrecy, Elisande told him about their plan for the night adding, "Tonight he may remember everything."

"God grant it's t'*right* everything," Parse was heard to mutter as he went on his way.

God grant it—Elisande muttered that prayer to

herself as they set out for Hanard House after supper. Their excuse—that it was so fine an evening that they wished to exercise Lord Raven's horses—apparently convinced Constance, who had sworn that she wanted nothing more to do with the fearsome beasts and had insisted that the mare she had ridden that day be returned to Lord Raven without delay.

Leaving Constance experimenting with a new tea, Elisande and Nigel, with Parse riding pillion, embarked on their journey. Apprehension at what the night might bring lengthened the way and darkened the shadows of the woods that hugged the side of the road. They left Parse off at his watch point near the foot of the hill, but Nigel, who had until now been in a froth of impatience, began to hang back.

"Come, Nigel—Anabelle is waiting for us," Elisande urged. As he still hesitated, she added, "The colonel isn't at home and Parse will be watching the road in case he returns."

"You don't think it's Hanard I fear?" Nigel hesitated to add, "Supposing I do remember what happened on March thirtieth—and I'm guilty as Cain?"

Without waiting for an answer, the young man spurred his horse and rode past Elisande up the path to the big house. Here a solitary groom came to take charge of the horses, and the colonel's lady herself opened the massive oaken door.

"I have sent all of the servants to a fair in Allford," she explained in a conspiratorial whisper. "The only two in the house are my personal groom and my abigail, and *they* are as trustworthy as your own man, Cap—I mean, Mr. Redding. Hugo will take good care of your horses, don't fear. Are you prepared?"

" 'Armed and well prepared,' " Nigel tried to

speak lightly, but a muscle twitched in his lean cheek. "I'm at your command, ma'am."

"On the contrary, it's I who wish to serve you, sir." Anabelle Hanard smiled kindly at the young man. "Will you have some refreshment first?"

But Nigel was too nervous to wait and asked if they could begin at once. "I'll tell you everything that I remember about that night," he said.

Elisande gnawed her lower lip as she watched her brother stride the length of the ground-floor hallway and pause at the foot of the stairs.

"I arrived at the house late—around nine," he began. "The colonel came out here to greet me. Told him I carried dispatches from the Duke of Wellington. He wanted to put them into the safe straightaway, so we went up to his study together."

"Perhaps," Elisande suggested, "if you *show* us what you did it will help you remember."

Nigel nodded and, followed by Elisande and Anabelle, mounted the stairs to the first floor. Here he paused at the open door of the great room, where the gaming party had been held. Candles were lit inside that deserted room, giving the armorial hangings an eerie look.

"Dancing was going on," Nigel mused. "Sylvia—Miss Hanard—was dancing. Looked so beautiful I couldn't take my eyes off her."

"But you followed Colonel Hanard up to his study," Elisande prompted him. "Where is that?"

The study was also on the second floor. Paneled in wood that had darkened over the ages, it was a large room with a closed-in secretive look. Framed maps, ponderous leather-bound books, portraits of the colonel's ancestors, and a marble bust of Nelson all gloomed over an enormous, leather-tooled desk.

Elisande and Anabelle stopped in the doorway as Nigel crossed the study and stopped before a canvas depicting Hercules slaying a lion. Swinging it aside, he disclosed a wall safe.

"The colonel unlocked the safe, put the dispatches in the safe, locked it. We spoke about Louis of France doing a bunk to Ghent, talked about the campaign to come. The colonel said he knew I'd conduct myself gallantly—"

Nigel's voice trailed away. "What then?" Elisande forced herself to ask.

With an effort, Nigel pulled himself together. "Both of us went back to the great room. Remember we met *you* in the hall, Mrs. Hanard. Colonel asked if you'd honor him by dancing the cotillion with him."

Anabelle pulled a droll face. "I *do* remember that. We danced the cotillion together, and the colonel trod on the train of my new gown and tore it, too. Shall we go back to the great room, now?"

She moved aside to let Nigel pass, but he did not move, and Elisande noted that her brother was staring fixedly at the books above the desk.

"The *Memoirs of Hadrian* is gone," he exclaimed. "It used to stand there, next to the Plato. The colonel kept his spare key in the *Hadrian*."

"A spare key to the safe, do you mean?" Anabelle exclaimed in surprise.

"No one knew about it except the colonel and myself. So that the book would lie flat, he carved out a piece inside the book to house the key."

Nigel paused to explain that the colonel used to carry his keys on his watch fob. "But he was absentminded sometimes, and when he forgot to wear the watch he didn't want to bother sending for it or fetching it himself. Ergo, the spare key in the book—"

Nigel broke off, blinked several times, and then shook his head. "What is it?" Elisande asked. "Did you remember something?"

"Thought so. There was something for a minute—gone now" was the unhappy reply. "Might as well go back to the great room now."

Battling her disappointment, Elisande followed Nigel and Anabelle back to the silent great room where Nigel had found Sylvia still dancing every dance. "I—I couldn't watch her in another man's arms," he said. "So, after a while I decided to go outside into the garden and blow a—I mean, smoke a cigar."

Silently the women followed him down the stairs and out of a side door. It was cool in the garden, and it had grown quite dark. Elisande almost jumped as Anabelle put a hand on her shoulder. "Look," she whispered. "See how still he stands."

Nigel had walked some distance away and was standing almost at attention. He seemed to be listening for a voice that only he could hear. Elisande held her breath as she watched her brother stand in that same rigid way for several minutes. But then he shook his head.

"It's no good," he added despairingly. "Again, there was *something* for a second—gone now. As though a wall came down inside my head, and I can't get past it no matter what I do."

Elisande could have wept with frustration, but the colonel's wife only said, "Don't give up so quickly, Mr. Redding. Why not walk about and let your mind clear of thoughts."

Obediently Nigel walked away into the garden toward a narrow path that lay near a grove of oak trees. "He is going to the Cliff Path." When Elisande looked puzzled, Anabelle explained, "The Cliff Path begins at the edge of the garden and leads through the woods to the cliffs behind the house."

"Perhaps he means to explore the cliffs?"

"Not without a lantern! Climbing down those

stone steps is difficult even in the daytime." Annabelle paused to shiver delicately. "But see—he has stopped walking."

Elisande sighed. "I am afraid he doesn't remember anything after all."

"Perhaps not tonight, but—Elisande, watch your brother carefully tomorrow and see if there is any change. He may not be aware of it, but you will see it."

"You sound like Lord Raven," Elisande sighed.

"Truly?" Anabelle sounded thoughtful as she asked, "Lord Raven has befriended your brother, hasn't he?"

"In a manner of speaking," Elisande replied absently. She was striving to make out Nigel's hazy form in the darkness.

"The Marquess Farmer told Cuthbert that he has called a truce in order to help Mr. Redding regain his memory," Anabelle Hanard continued. "He mumbled something about allowing Sylvia to have her choice of suitors, but I don't believe a word of it. I am persuaded that the marquess would do anything to discredit his rival and believes that his brother is helping him."

She turned to look full at Elisande. "But I'm persuaded that Raven is playing another game entirely."

Constance was wrong, Elisande thought. Mrs. Hanard was no empty-headed rattle. "Lord Raven feels that the marquess and Miss Hanard will not suit," she said. "He hopes that if Nigel can prove his innocence, the marquess will give up his courtship."

The colonel's wife laughed her silvery laugh. "Lud, so that is it. I had thought—"

"What did you think?" Elisande questioned as the colonel's wife broke off in midsentence.

"Raven has the reputation of being an adventurer, my dear. His sort craves excitement and change. He's obviously bored in Dorset, so I expected he would look for a diversion."

Elisande felt a dull jab under her breastbone. *Diversion,* her mind hissed derisively. *That is all you were to his lordship!*

Aloud she said, "That is not the case at all."

"I should have guessed that you are too sensible to be taken in by a plump-pursed rogue with a handsome face. A good thing, my dear. You might have lived to regret it—as several other foolish females have no doubt done."

Anabelle checked herself and laughed ruefully. "Lud," she apologized, "I sound like a gabble-monger, don't I? But as your friend I feel that I must warn you—go carefully. For all his wealth and his noble blood, Lord Raven is no gentleman. Once your brother ceases to be of use to him, milord will cast him aside like a shopworn cloak."

And he will cast you aside, too. "Thank you for the warning," Elisande said quietly, "but I know that already."

"As I said, you are wise for your years. I, unfortunately, was widowed at a very young age, and Graymount left me no money." Anabelle's silvery voice grew uncharacteristically harsh as she went on, "The world is a terrible place for a young female with good looks and empty pockets, my dear. Perhaps I will shock you when I say that I received many a carte blanche from men like Lord Raven before dear Cuthbert offered for me."

She broke off as approaching footsteps signaled Nigel's return. "Ah, Captain Redding," she called. "Have you remembered anything at all?"

Elisande's heart sank as her brother shook his head. She could not see his face in the dim light, but his voice was bleak with despair as he said, "Nothing, ma'am. Sorry to report that after all the trouble you've gone through on my behalf, I remember nothing."

Dark hair, darker than the shadows. And horns. Those golden horns. Who are you?

"Captain, sir, wake up. Tha'rt dreaming again!"

Can't see your face. Turn around and look at me. Turn, damn it! Laughing at me. Cruel laughter. Familiar laughter, somehow—

"Nigel—Nigel, please try and wake up. Parse, if he thrashes about like this he will injure himself."

Where are you going? I mean to follow you. But where are you going? This is an evil place. Woman, where are you taking me?

"Nay, sir, I don't want to do this. Forgive me."

Nigel sat bolt upright in bed as Parse sponged icy water all over his face. As his hazy consciousness returned, he realized that he was in his bed, that Elisande was holding him by one arm, and Constance by the other. Both women looked frightened.

"Oh, my God," he groaned. "Why did you wake me up?"

Elisande said nothing. Constance gruffed, "You were screaming and writhing, Nigel, and fighting all of us. We feared you would do harm to yourself."

"It was t'old nightmare, only ten times worse," white-faced Parse added.

"If you hadn't awakened me, I might have seen what *she* looked like." Almost desperately Nigel turned to his sister. "Lisa, I was in the garden at Hanard House. I was looking for the colonel, but then *she* came. Laughed at me and dared me to follow her."

"Who was *she*?" Elisande caught her brother's hands in hers. "Who, Nigel?"

He shook his head miserably. "I don't know."

"Tha were shouting something about horns," Parse suggested helpfully.

"Yes, that's it—remember the horns, now. Strange-looking things—bright, as if they were made of gold." Nigel frowned in terrible concentration. "No, not horns," he said at last. "Combs. Couldn't see her face, but I did see those golden combs stuck in her hair. You know the ones I mean, don't you, Lisa? The kind that Spanish women wear."

Chapter Six

"Spanish combs. Now, who would wear Spanish combs?"

Elisande stopped to evade a large puddle of water in the middle of the village street. It had rained last night, and Camston-on-Sea was a mine field of ruts and potholes. As she made her wary progress through the muck, Elisande laid aside the puzzle of the combs for a moment in order to balance her heavy market basket whilst keeping Constance's cloak out of the mud.

The rain had brought both a chill wind and the scent of the sea, and while Con's coat was too short for her, it was warmer than her own. Elisande shivered against the cutting wind and tried to ignore the smell of salt. It reminded her too much of Lord Raven.

His lordship had not manifested himself since the day of their outing to the Norman Church, but the memory of his kisses was too real for comfort. Once more Elisande forced herself to concentrate on matters at hand. She had come out to do the marketing since Parse was out riding with Nigel, and she needed to make a decision. Beef bones would cost less and go further in a soup eked out with barley and vegetables. Still, Nigel needed meat.

He had looked so pale this morning. Since their unsuccessful foray to Hanard House, he seemed consumed with nervous energy, and Parse reported that the captain had not had one good night's sleep. No food, no rest—and he was not talking much either. He would break off in the middle of a sentence to stare into the distance with unseeing eyes.

Elisande's thoughts were interrupted as a group of village children scampered by. They were shouting to each other and pointing toward a small but animated crowd that had gathered near the millpond some distance away, and as they ran one of them shrilled, "You, Joe—go get 'Arriet—quick!"

On the heels of this command came raucous laughter and a man's rough voice demanding, "Well, wot d'you say? How long can the little bleeder stay afloat?"

There were various answering shouts, as well as vociferous protests that such a bet was a waste of good brass. "The beast's going to drown afore you even gets the bets down," someone shouted.

Curious, Elisande walked toward the crowd. It was hard to see over so many heads, but by standing on tiptoe she could make out something bobbing about in the center of the millpond. It resembled a sodden blob of gray cotton.

"Garn, you bugger—swim fer it," shouted a large, hairy personage dressed in a bottle-green coat and rough workman's breeches. He had a dirty yellow cloth tied around his neck and a sparkling gold ring on his finger. A prominent gold tooth flashed as he added, "I've got a silver feeder on you."

"I tell yer, Ned, 'e ain't never going to make it ter shore."

To Elisande's horror, the sodden blob in the middle of the pond turned and began scrabbling with its paws. Simultaneously, a familiar, shrill voice erupted nearby. "Halexander!" Harriet Willoughby wailed. "Oh, Halexander! Wot're you doing to my dog?"

The man in green showed long yellow teeth in a sneer. " 'E ain't yours no more. That slumguzzling beast ate me bread and cheese, and I'm going to take me lunch out of 'is mangy 'ide."

Five or six louts who were loitering around guffawed, and one of them called, "A shilling says 'e won't last more'n a minute longer, Ned."

Once more the air was rife with speculation. Harriet tried to go to her pet's rescue but was held back by one of the louts, who grinned, "Yer 'eard Ned. Shut your gob, young'un, or I'll pitch yer into the pond, too."

Harriet began to wail. Alexander almost reached the shore but was kicked back into midpond by the man with the gold tooth. "You bully," Elisande cried, but her voice was drowned in the yells of the now excited crowd, which was placing bets on how long the dog would survive.

She looked around her and recognized a man who lived near Willoughby Cottage. "Help me put a stop to this cruel business," she pleaded.

The man avoided her eyes and muttered that he was sick and tired of young 'Arriet's mangy mongrel, which was always getting into his chicken coop. Others standing nearby nodded agreement, and Elisande wondered what she should do. Of course she could try and get help, but that help might come too late for Alexander.

There was nothing else to do. Elisande set down her basket and removed her shoes. Then she pushed her way through the crowd until she stood on the edge of the pond.

" 'Oy, there—what d'you think you're doing?" the man with the gold tooth yelped as Elisande stepped into the water. Ignoring him, she called to Alexander meanwhile trying to keep her balance on the slippery mud underfoot.

"Gerrout o' this," Gold Tooth bellowed. "You, Mingus—stop 'er!"

A fellow with a flat, vicious face strode up to the water's edge and reached for Elisande. She swung out of his reach, and he lost his balance and fell into the millpond.

"Alexander," she called urgently, "come to me."

Eyes rolling in its head, the little dog began to swim toward Elisande. She could hear its exhausted gasps as it swam, and also the curses of the man called Mingus behind her. "When I get me fambles on you, you'll be sorry you was never born," he swore.

Elisande's heart was beating hard as she scooped Alexander out of the water and started to wade toward the bank where Gold Tooth was practically dancing with temper. "Mingus, wot are you waiting for?" he raved. "Take that dog haway from that trollop and throw 'im back in the drink."

"Who are you calling a trollop?" All the frustrations and worries of the past few weeks erupted into indignation as Elisande whirled to face the dripping Mingus. "If you lay a hand on me or on this animal," she threatened, "you will be the sorriest man in England."

Astonished at her defiance as well as by her cultured speech, the man hesitated. "How dare you call me a trollop!" Elisande went on furiously. "You are all criminals. You stole this poor animal from Harriet Willoughby."

" 'At's a lie," Gold Tooth was beginning hotly when a blob of mud hit him in the face.

"Good 'un, Joe—you got 'im!" Harriet shrieked.

Jerking out of the grip of the man who was holding her, she bent down, scooped up some mud, and let fly at Mingus. It hit him square on the nose.

"C'mon, you lot," Harriet whooped, "let's get them barstids!"

With yells of glee, the village urchins joined in the fray, and soon missiles of every description were sailing through the air. Gold Tooth and his bully boys were pelted with mud, stones, sticks, and refuse. "Gerrout of 'ere," Harriet hooted. "You ain't wanted. Thieves! We'll get the law on yer!"

Amidst the uproar, Elisande made her way to shore. She set the sodden Alexander down and ruefully noted that she was nearly as wet as he. Her stockings were soaking, her skirts and cloak bordered with mud. *Con will scold,* she thought bleakly.

It was Constance's only cloak, and the sopping hose were her warmest stockings. Elisande shivered suddenly as cold from her drenched hose invaded the rest of her body and knew that if she wore them all the way home, she might catch a chill.

There was a flat rock by the pond. It was shaded from the road, and besides everybody's attention was taken up by Harriet's battle with Gold Tooth and his ruffians. Elisande squelched over to the rock, sat down, and rolling down one stocking, popped it into her basket.

"Well, this is beyond everything!"

The scandalized, breathless little voice was vaguely familiar. Elisande looked up from removing her second stocking and saw that a handsome barouche had stopped on the road a few yards away. A lady was leaning out of her conveyance and staring at her through a quizzing glass.

The outraged, sharp little face under the cloud of frizzy red hair brought unpleasant memories. "Good God," Elisande exclaimed. "Lady Carme."

Lady Carme's eyes narrowed. Her mean little mouth pursed. "Yes, Miss Redding, it is I." With profound satisfaction she added, "I thought that I saw you emerging from amongst that disgusting mob. That you would consort with such raff and chaff is in itself the outside of enough, but to remove your *stockings* in public—it is an *outrage*, miss. What have you to say for yourself?"

Never apologize, never explain. Unaccountably Lord Raven's maxim slid into Elisande's mind. Calmly she slid on her shoes and rose to confront the outraged lady in the barouche.

"Are you enjoying Dorset, ma'am?" she asked politely.

Lady Carme looked ready to explode. "I shall be forever thankful that I did not let my kind heart— and the fact that poor Hortense was my friend— overtake my good sense. If I had employed you, it would have been a disaster. Not only are you related to a traitor, but you yourself are debased!"

Elisande could see three small faces peering around their mother. Their eyes were bright with malicious curiosity, and one of them stuck out her tongue. "Indeed, we must be thankful," Elisande agreed.

Behind her, Harriet's triumphant screeches were urging the retreating "barstids" to reside in hell. My lady shivered and begged her offspring to cover their ears. Then she resumed, "Miss Redding, words cannot express my outrage. You are not fit to associate with decent people—"

"Can you ever forgive me, ma'am?"

Lady Carme whipped around, and Elisande stared as Lord Raven drew his curricle up to the side of the road. He tossed his reins to his groom, descended, and strode forward saying, "I know that I'm late. Mrs. Hanard will be furious at me for not collecting you in time for luncheon."

Elisande blinked hard. Was he speaking to *her*?

"Come, Miss Redding." Lord Raven bowed

slightly and offered his arm. "The ladies are expecting us at Hanard House."

Lady Carme had been frozen with astonishment. Now she came to life with a jerk. "You are taking this—this female to Hanard House?" she gabbled. "But—but I had heard—it is said that the colonel will not receive this woman or her treacherous brother."

As if he had only now realized her presence, Lord Raven slowly turned his head. For a long, cold moment he regarded my lady. "Ah, Lady Carme," he said at last.

The fact that icicles hung from his lordship's voice was not lost on Lady Carme, who flushed, fidgeted, and finally pulled herself together enough to simper, "Good day, dear Lord Raven. I am here, you know, for the—the wedding. As Mrs. Colonel Hanard's dear friend, I was shocked to hear about the terrible business that has postponed—"

Lord Raven interrupted her smoothly. "Forgive me, but Mrs. Hanard has been expecting Miss Redding this past hour. Perkins will take the basket, Miss Redding. If you're comfortably bestowed, we'll be off. Good day to you, madam."

Completely bewildered, Elisande allowed herself to be carried off. "That," Lord Raven explained, "is what they mean by *deus ex machina*."

"Where did you come from?" Elisande demanded.

"I was riding through the village and heard the commotion. I'm glad I was able to save you from that toadeating griffin, though unfortunately I was too late to interfere with your heroics. Nigel isn't going to thank you for rescuing Harriet Willoughby's wretched mongrel."

His light eyes were amused, and the humor of the situation suddenly caught up with Elisande. She began a chuckle that turned into a full laugh as she recollected Lady Carme's pop-eyed expression.

After anger and frustration, laughter was a relief. She laughed until the tears came, and Lord Raven raised a quizzical eyebrow. "Are you laughing or crying?"

"Laughing—I think." She pulled her handkerchief from her pocket and wiped her eyes determinedly, but the tears still pooled in her eyes and slid down her cheeks. "I don't know what's wrong with me," she confessed.

Looking at her sideways, Raven saw the dark shadows under her clear eyes and understood the pressures that had been weighing hard on Elisande Redding's slender shoulders. It was not a bit of his concern, of course, but even so it was difficult not to admire her spirit or to want to comfort her—

Lord Raven gave himself a mental shake and stared hard at the road directly in front of him. "You're a brave woman," he said abruptly.

His change of tone served to dry her tears. Elisande drew a steadying breath and managed to gulp down the knot in her throat. "Not at all," she said almost steadily. "The pond is really quite shallow, and Harriet's army of friends was there to defend me."

Leave it alone—best not to get into deep waters, Raven reminded himself. In a lighter tone he said, "So Alexander had another brush with disaster. I don't doubt someone *will* drown him if he doesn't mend his ways. He and his mistress aren't popular with the villagers."

"Harriet is very young," Elisande pointed out.

"Actually, I admire her spirit. It must have been hard to see her father go off to war. He raised her more as a son than a daughter, but when it was time to march away with the soldiers, he left her at home with the other women."

She looked at him in surprise. "You are well informed," she exclaimed.

Broad shoulders shrugged. "It's a very small village."

The cynicism in his voice recalled what Anabelle had said about Lord Raven. Not for one moment did she believe what he had said about chancing to drive by this morning. Very little this gentleman did was by chance.

"Has the marquess changed his mind about marrying Miss Hanard?" she probed.

"Unfortunately, no. Once Wigram gets a notion in his brain, it stays there until dislodged by sheer force. And you? Has Nigel remembered anything?"

"Nothing that makes sense—" Elisande broke off to ask, "Why are we going this way, my lord?"

It had just occurred to her that they had left the village and were driving down the common road. Before them lay the fork in the road. "Surely we aren't really going to Hanard House?" she asked in some alarm.

He shook his head. "After your morning's activities I thought you might enjoy a ride. Besides, we need to talk, Madam Ally. I've heard that Nigel has been riding all over Dorset as if the devil himself was at his coattails. What unimportant thing did he remember?"

Instead of answering, Elisande looked around her and saw that they were passing the Norman Church. And beyond the big, gray edifice mostly hidden amongst old oaks, the landscape seemed to change. Instead of trees, furze grew in tufts on the sandy ground and the sound of the sea was much closer.

"I did not realize how far we had come," Elisande said. "Pray turn back—Con will be worried about me. I will tell you about Nigel on the way back to Willoughby Cottage."

"But are you sure you want to turn back immediately? The sea is on the other side of those dunes." Lord Raven pointed with his whip. "Wouldn't you like a glimpse of it?"

As he spoke, he guided his curricle onto a pathway that threaded through the dunes, and Elisande involuntarily caught her breath. Before her lay a vast expanse of water over which sailed puffy white clouds. Some distance away to the northwest rose jagged stone cliffs, while toward the east a curve of sand formed a cove. A boat was moored at the long stone pier that extended out into the calm blue water.

"This is Swan's Cove," Lord Raven explained. Then, seeing Elisande glance sharply toward the rocks, he added, "Yes—Hanard House stands above those cliffs."

Elisande noted that steps had been cut in the gray rock face. "The Hanards' Cliff Path," she mused. "Is that the only way to reach the cove?"

"No. I was told that throughout the years smugglers used the deep waters hereabouts to make landfall. The locals still use the 'smuggler's road' that cuts through the Hanards' woods to Swan's Cove." Lord Raven paused. "This is where your brother supposedly handed over Wellington's dispatches to the French."

Elisande knew that she should feel chilled by this knowledge, but the fact was that there was nothing menacing about Swan's Cove. "How beautiful the ocean is," she sighed.

"Haven't you ever seen the sea before?" he asked, surprised.

"Not like this. Of course I have seen it off and on since coming to Dorset, and when Nigel and I were children our parents took us to Brighton. But somehow this is different." She looked around her and added softly, "And you have sailed on this ocean—sailed out of sight over that horizon."

He was watching her face as he agreed, "Over many horizons."

Then, abruptly, he swung down from his curricle. "What are you doing?" Elisande asked in surprise.

"Don't deny that you're standing there wondering how it feels to be out there in a boat," was his reply. "There's not time like the present to find out."

Lord Raven nodded to the sailboat moored by the pier. "Come, Miss Redding. Let me lead you into temptation."

His deep voice caressed a memory that was both uncomfortable and irresistible. She stood on perilous ground, Elisande knew. "I—do not think that would be wise," she began. "Con is waiting for me, and—"

"Surely Miss Dayton will understand." He was smiling persuasively at her, his eyes the exact color of the sea. "You were the one who yearns for adventure," he reminded her softly. "But perhaps you have changed your mind?"

A puff of sea wind caught Elisande's ancient bonnet and set it straining against its ribbons. The sailboat glistened in the sun, the sea beckoned. Elisande drew a deep breath and said, "No, I haven't changed your mind."

"Then, come." He held out his hands to her, and without listening to the alarm bells that were clanging and clamoring in her brain, Elisande took those strong, cool hands and was swung down to the ground. For a second he held her close to him, but then he let her go and turned to give an order to his groom.

"Perkins will help launch us," Lord Raven explained as they walked toward the pier. "I'll be the captain and you will be the crew. Agreed?"

"But I know nothing about sailing—"

Elisande broke off as they stepped onto the pier. When she looked over the side, she could see her distorted reflection in the water. For an instant she found herself thinking about Nigel and the disturbing images in his dreams. Then they came up to the boat and all other thoughts vanished.

"Ready, Miss Redding?" Lord Raven asked. She nodded resolutely, and he climbed into the boat and held out his hands to help her down. "Easy does it—let Perkins assist you. There's nothing to fear."

Elisande did not feel in the least bit afraid. Excitement, pleasure, anticipation, all brimmed in her as she took her seat in the boat. Perkins loosed the rope that secured the craft to its moorings, and it floated gently out to sea.

Entranced, Elisande watched as Lord Raven raised the sail. When the crinkled canvas hung limp for a second and then puffed out proudly as the wind caught it, she could not help applauding. This was what she had dreamed of, imagined, for so long.

"Do you want to try and steer?" Lord Raven asked when they were fairly on their way. "It's not hard to do. Push the tiller to one side, and the boat will move in the opposite direction. If you push the tiller down, the rudder will turn the boat into the wind. If you want to turn off from the wind, push the tiller up."

He broke off as, without the slightest hesitation, Elisande scrambled up beside him and took the tiller in her hands. "Steady as she goes, Captain?" she questioned happily.

"Steady as she goes, ma'am. The wind is at our back and we are running free."

She nodded, and he watched her absorbed face thoughtfully. Elisande Redding, Raven told himself, was not really beautiful. Other women he had known had been prettier, more witty, infinitely richer. Yet, he could scarcely recall their faces or their names whereas he had the sense that he would somehow always remember Elisande with her face turned toward the sea and enchantment in her eyes.

"How do you like steering?" he forced himself to ask.

"I love it. Truly, I do. It is so wonderful to cut ties with everything landlocked and solid and to *run free*." Elisande paused. "I am glad that you brought me out here on this boat. Is it yours?"

He shook his head. "It belongs to Hanard. He knows I enjoy sailing and put this boat at my disposal." Lord Raven then heard himself adding, "Someday I'll take you on the *Silver Raven* and you'll see what real sailing is."

The wind shifted as he spoke, and Elisande somewhat reluctantly relinquished her post. As Raven brought the sailboat about and sent it running free again, he realized that he felt more relaxed and happier than he had for as long as he could remember. It was no wonder, after all—he had not been on the sea for many months.

"Tell me about the *Silver Raven*," Elisande said after a moment's contented silence. "Is she beautiful?"

"When it comes into port under full sail, there's no better sight," he replied. "Below deck, the forward and after cabins are appointed in silver velvet and dark rosewood. And the figurehead was especially carved for me by American Indians. It shows a raven with a silver globe in its mouth."

"Meaning that when you sail her, you command the world," Elisande mused. He looked surprised at her perception as she added, "No wonder you miss her and—oh, look there! Are those really swans?"

Following her gaze, Raven saw that a pair of

large, white birds were floating on the gentle swells. "They nest in a marsh nearby. That's where the cove got its name," he explained.

The birds swam up to within a few feet of the boat. They arched their long necks and looked curiously at Elisande and then suddenly took wing and flew away.

As Elisande leaned back to see the birds' flight, her hair brushed Raven's cheek. Over the scent of the sea he drew in her fragrance. Involuntarily, mindlessly, his arms closed about her.

Elisande felt herself drawn backward against Lord Raven's hard chest. She felt the strength of his arms pressing her close against him, his cool cheek against hers. If she turned her head even slightly, her lips would meet his.

She knew that she should protest, needed to protest—and could not. She could not even breathe. Remembered fire slid through her and stole the power of reasoning from her mind and strength from her limbs. Only her heart was moving—beating and beating like a wild thing as she slowly, irresistibly, turned her face to meet his kiss.

There was a sudden flap of sail, a jerking of the boat. Elisande cried out as she was almost flung out of Lord Raven's arms. "What has happened?" she gasped.

"Wind shift," he explained, steadying her. "Don't worry—I'll bring us about."

Elisande blinked back to reality as Lord Raven accomplished this. She felt shaken and a little frightened, but not because of anything that the boat had done. Once again being with Lord Raven had made her actually forget Nigel's plight. And this was after she had boasted to Anabelle Hanard that she was not going to be taken in by his lordship's charm.

But now she had remembered—now she was herself again. "We were going to talk about Nigel," she reminded him as the boat began to run free again.

Raven recognized the shift in her voice and congratulated himself on once again avoiding danger. He listened attentively as Elisande detailed the experiment that she and the colonel's wife had conducted and of Nigel's nightmare until she concluded, "But now he is worse. I was wrong to suggest going to Hanard House. I should have listened to Con's cards and stayed in Sussex."

The anxious tremor in her voice and his own instinctive response to it made Lord Raven frown. *Deep waters,* he reminded himself and hastily deflected the talk to a safer subject. "Surely you don't believe in Miss Dayton's fortune-telling?" he asked.

"No, but Con believes in her tarot cards, and I respect that." Seeing Lord Raven shrug, she added somewhat defensively, "When Con was growing up, she was so shy that she had few friends, and after her mother died, she was even more alone. She turned to her herbs and teas and the tarot for companionship."

"What about her father?" Lord Raven asked in a way that clearly asked, why did *he* tolerate such nonsense?

"My uncle Dayton cared for nothing except his horses and his gaming," Elisande replied bluntly. "In the end he gambled away everything, even Con's inheritance." She paused to add, "I beg you will not scoff at Constance, my lord. I am sure you have seen marvels on your travels that seemed like magic."

"Ah, but they only *seemed* like magic," Lord Raven pointed out. "Everything has a logical explanation." He seemed about to say more, then checked himself and looked thoughtfully at Elisande. "Perhaps," he mused. "Perhaps it would work. This might be the right time."

"I beg your pardon?" Elisande asked.

"I was thinking that it's time to return you to dry land," Lord Raven said. "Miss Dayton will be starting to worry about you."

Their return to the pier was a silent one. Lord Raven seemed sunk in a brown study, and Elisande watched the horizon melting into the sky and remembered the swans she had seen. It was true that the sea cast a spell, she thought. Perhaps it had been that witchery that had made her so susceptible to Lord Raven's charm—

"Miss Redding."

Elisande started as his deep voice interrupted her reverie. "You mentioned that your brother's mysterious lady wore Spanish combs," Lord Raven went on. "I've just remembered a remark Mrs. Hanard made the night of the card party at Hanard House. She said that she wished she had her stepdaughter's golden combs to use as a wager."

Elisande looked up eagerly. "And you think she could have meant *Spanish* combs?"

"It's easy enough to find out." Lord Raven drew the boat alongside the pier, tossed a rope to his groom, and added, "We'll drive to Hanard House and ask the lady."

"I doubt if the colonel will welcome me," she pointed out.

"He would welcome *me*," Lord Raven said firmly. "And he would welcome my guest. Think of it— perhaps the answer to Nigel's problems is waiting for you at Hanard House."

Elisande nodded resolutely. "We will go—but first I must change. My first encounter with water today was less pleasant than the second."

Though she spoke lightly, she was heavyhearted as Lord Raven handed her onto the pier. Out there amongst the waves and the swans, she had felt happy. Now, back on dry ground, all her old burdens and worries were clustering about her once more.

When they returned to Willoughby Cottage, an unfamiliar trap stood before the door. Lord Raven looked astonished. "By all that's holy, what's Wigram doing here?"

"He has come to continue the quarrel he and Nigel began the other day," Elisande exclaimed nervously. But when she hurried inside the cottage, she saw that her brother was nowhere to be seen and that Constance and the little marquess were sitting on either side of the fire, talking amicably.

They looked up as Elisande came in, and the marquess bounced to his feet explaining, "I, er—came to return Miss Dayton's handkerchief and tell Redding that even after the other day I mean to hold to the truce."

In a loud aside he added, "I say, Ivo, what do you think of *my* plan? Decided I'd pretend to bear the olive branch and see if I could smoke that blackguard out myself. Deuced clever, ain't I?"

Meanwhile, a pink-cheeked Constance was telling Elisande, "It is so blustery outside, so I offered the marquess my mixture of chamomile and orange blossoms sweetened with—oh heavens, dearest—your skirt! What has happened?"

Leaving Lord Raven to explain, Elisande hastened to her room to change out of her muddied garment and into her walking-out dress. When she emerged, she found Lord Raven standing by the fire and looking profoundly bored whilst his brother was expounding on his plans for an apiary at Tanner Place.

"I always wanted an apiary," he was telling Constance dreamily. "Capital things, bees. Buzzin' around and makin' bang-up honey and mindin' the flowers. Always liked 'em."

"Indeed, I have always believed that an apiary is an excellent thing," Constance agreed earnestly. "Imagine making one's own honey and not having to rely on the local supply—which is often far from adequate. I have read three books about the subject."

"No, have you? I say, that's fascinatin'," the marquess exclaimed. "Truly astonishin' coincidence, us both likin' bees. Deuced astonishin'."

Lord Raven signaled with his eyes toward the door. As Elisande gathered up her cloak, Constance and the marquess had their heads close together. "No one else will take him seriously," Lord Raven said as they went outside. "Your cousin's a kind woman."

Elisande looked doubtfully back at the cottage. "Is it wise to leave your brother here? If Nigel returns, there might be a confrontation."

"No fear of that. As Wigram himself told me, he's come bearing the olive branch."

While he was speaking, Lord Raven caught himself wondering how Elisande might look in fashionable clothes and a bonnet that was not suited to a dowager of ninety. "Forget about my brother and think instead of yours," he directed. "You are sure that Nigel has never mentioned these Spanish combs before this?"

Elisande shook her head. "But even if Miss Hanard *does* have Spanish combs, where will that lead us?"

Into temptation. The words brushed Raven's mind for a second before he dismissed them impatiently. Now was not the time for idiocy. What Miss Elisande Redding thought, said, or wore was all one to him as long as he could tear Wigram loose from his abominable fixation and shake the dust of Dorset from his feet.

"That is defeatist thinking," he said abruptly. "As I've told you, there is always a solution to a problem. We only have to find it."

But *where* to find it? Elisande was deep in thought as they drove toward Hanard House where, she was relieved to discover, the colonel had ridden out. Anabelle and Sylvia were sitting in the conservatory, and the colonel's wife welcomed them with her usual vivacity.

"You see before you a most miserable woman," she called cheerfully. "I lost a great deal at piquet last night—mostly to that dreadful woman, Lady Carme. You are right, Elisande. Never, never take up gaming. And you, Sylvia, be warned by my example."

Sylvia Hanard shrugged. "I don't care for gambling."

Elisande saw that Miss Hanard did not look her lovely self this morning. Her skin was more pale than creamy, and her eyes had a dissatisfied, restless look.

"I didn't sleep well," she replied petulantly in answer to Elisande's polite inquiry. "All that rain kept me awake, and when I wanted to ride out this morning, Papa was as cross as crabs. He won't let me set foot outside the house, so I have had no exercise at all today."

"Then perhaps you'll walk with me now," Lord Raven suggested, smiling and offering his arm.

Sylvia, Elisande noted, was not impervious to Lord Raven's smile. As they strolled away, Anabelle pulled her chair closer to Elisande. "Well?" she whispered. "Tell me at once. What has happened?"

When Elisande had recounted Nigel's dream, the colonel's lady looked disappointed. "Oh, lud, is that all?" she exclaimed. "Unfortunately, that's easily explained. Sylvia wore a black-and-gold Spanish dress that night and the combs that Cuthbert brought her from Spain. Captain Redding is probably only remembering how handsome she looked."

"I suspect that you are right." Elisande looked across the conservatory to where Miss Hanard was talking and laughing with Lord Raven.

She did not look as if she had a care in the world, Elisande thought drearily. In spite of her dramatic protestations, Sylvia would forget about Nigel the moment another and better offer presented itself. Perhaps she had already forgotten about him. "And he cannot forget about her even in his dreams," she muttered.

"Don't despair, Elisande," Anabelle said sympathetically. "Your brother said that it was as if there were a curtain through which he could not see. Once a corner of the curtain is raised, there's hope that one day he'll remember everything."

"Nigel is trying so hard to remember that he may push himself too hard." Elisande clasped her hands tight in her lap to stop them from trembling. "Anabelle, I'm afraid for him."

The colonel's wife looked thoughtful for a moment and then suggested, "Why not ask Sylvia about the combs? Perhaps she can tell you something that might help."

At this moment Lord Raven and Miss Hanard came strolling back. The color had returned to Sylvia's cheeks, and she was laughing. "Lord Raven is such a shocking quiz," she commented in a much more cheerful tone. "So different from the marquess, who drives me silly with his fidgets."

Unfeeling little cat, Elisande thought. Aloud she said, "I need to ask a question, Miss Hanard. Do you remember wearing your Spanish combs on—on the night those military dispatches were stolen?"

"My what?" Sylvia Hanard asked. She sounded quite bored.

When Elisande explained, Sylvia gave a massive yawn and then asked indifferently, "Would you like to see the combs, Miss Redding? I'll show them to you if you come to my room."

She led the way out of the conservatory and up the stairs to a room on the third floor. An abigail jumped from the window seat where she had been sewing and curtsied, and Sylvia ordered her to bring in her small tortoiseshell jewelry box.

Once the box had been brought, Miss Hanard dismissed the girl and herself opened the box to display a set of golden combs sparkling with diamonds.

"I wore those combs only a short while," she said. "They were so heavy they gave me the headache. In fact, right after the first set that night, I went to lie down." She pushed the box from her adding carelessly, "I haven't worn them since."

When the light caught the diamonds, they gave off rays of light. Elisande felt a crushing disappointment. Anabelle Hanard had been right—Nigel had only been dreaming of Sylvia.

"He didn't remember anything of importance then," she sighed.

"How can you say that?" Sylvia tossed her head. "He remembered *me*."

The girl's conceit was beyond everything. Elisande got to her feet and said coldly, "I won't take any more of your time."

But before she could turn away, Sylvia reached out a hand to stop her. "Please don't go away. I am so *unhappy*," she said. Then she burst into tears.

Elisande stared in astonishment. Gone was the sulky, spoiled beauty of a moment ago. Miss Hanard's large emerald eyes swam with tears, her soft lips quivered. "Oh, I can't pretend not to care anymore," she sobbed. "Nigel thinks of me because I think of him. He dreams of me because I always dream of him, too."

"But you told him that you never wanted to see him again," Elisande protested.

"I didn't know what else to say. I *offered* to go away with him—to do anything he wanted," Sylvia Hanard wailed. "Do you think I would have waited a whole year—with Papa demanding every week that I accept some other odious suitor's offer—if I hadn't loved Nigel with all my heart?"

The hard knot of dislike in Elisande's heart had begun to melt, but she was still suspicious. Sylvia Hanard's moods were too changeable to be completely trusted. "You did agree to marry the marquess," she pointed out.

"Only because Papa is in dun territory," Sylvia replied with daunting honesty. "The fat little marquess is as rich as golden ball, and Papa needs a rich son-in-law to frank stepmama's gaming losses. Since Nigel had not written one letter to me—or so I thought then—I didn't much care *who* I married."

She squeezed Elisande's hands tightly. "I dare say that I'm selfish to a fault," she cried passionately, "but I do love Nigel, and if only he were mine, I would be sweet and loving and make life heaven on earth for him."

Somehow Elisande doubted it, but this was not the time for a debate on character. Meeting frankness with frankness she said, "If you love Nigel as you say, you must stop tormenting him by pretending you hate him. He needs to be calm if he's ever to regain his memory."

"Help me to meet him alone," Sylvia pleaded, "and I swear to you I'll put his mind at ease."

Elisande said bluntly, "Miss Hanard, if the colonel ever finds out that you have met my brother, all of us will be in the soup."

"Pooh!" Miss Hanard brushed such trifling considerations aside. "Call me Sylvia, because one day we will be sisters. Oh, Elisande, I promise I will be careful. I'll come to the meeting without a groom or abigail, and Papa will never, ever know. Won't you *please* help me arrange a meeting?"

Elisande weighed the risks and possible benefits of such a tryst. Lord Raven had said that every problem had a solution. Could a reconciliation with his lady love be the key that unlocked Nigel's memory?

Perhaps, she thought. Aloud she said, "But you must promise me that there will be no scenes. Nigel is so close to the edge now that any theatrics might push him past return." She looked sternly into Miss Hanard's vivid face. "Sylvia, I must have your word or I won't lift a finger."

Sylvia frowned and for a moment looked haughty and rebellious. Then she nodded quite meekly.

"You're right, and I'll do exactly as you say. Why would I do anything to hurt Nigel, Elisande? He's the only man I'll ever love."

Chapter Seven

"Where could Nigel have got to?"

Impatiently Elisande scanned the village road. "What can he be thinking of, being late *today* of all days? He knows we must be on our way by eleven."

"Perhaps it's as well that you don't go out riding together," Constance suggested from her place by the hearth. "I am persuaded that it will begin raining again soon."

It had been drizzling off and on all morning—a gloomy and unpropitious day for a tryst, Elisande conceded, but there was no help for it. And since it had taken a full week to arrange a time when the colonel would be out of the way, her brother could at least be on time to meet his Sylvia.

Since she had told him her plan, Nigel had been impossible to live with. One moment high in hope the next plunged in despair, he had driven his sister and their cousin wild. Even Parse, who seldom complained, had taken to muttering under his breath that he'd never expected the captain to act so "gormless."

And then, after everything had been finally arranged and they were to meet in the woods near the Norman Church at a quarter past eleven, Nigel had apparently had an attack of the nerves. Near dawn he had ridden off with Parse and had not yet returned.

"Perhaps he has changed his mind about meeting

Miss Hanard," Constance suggested. "It may be for the best. My cards warn that 'the way will be difficult,' so perhaps you will meet the colonel on the road—or the marquess. Truce or no, if *he* finds his betrothed trysting with Nigel, there will be trouble."

"Lord Raven has taken his brother to Allford for the day," Elisande said. "Besides, this is no ordinary tryst. It may help Nigel's memory."

"Is that what Lord Raven says?" Constance asked, and Elisande frowned as she recalled his lordship's reaction to her plan.

"I don't like it," he had said bluntly. "This rendezvous is just an excuse for more drama. Sylvia will weep and tear her hair like a tragedienne at Astley's Amphitheater, and Nigel will return home as sick as a horse. He'll be as far from remembering as he is now."

"It does seem a somewhat smoky plan," Elisande had agreed worriedly, "but I hoped that perhaps—"

"What *I'd* hoped was that Sylvia Hanard had lent those damned combs of hers to someone or lost them or sold them," Raven had interrupted. "Then there might have been a new trail to follow." He had then added somewhat ungraciously, "Well, if you've promised to act as chaperon, you have to go through with it. I'll keep Wigram out of the way."

Elisande winced at the memory. She herself had several grave doubts about today's meeting and would have canceled it if she could. But Sylvia had been determined that the tryst take place, and up till now Nigel had been as eager as his beloved.

"Where *is* he?" Elisande wondered.

Just then there was a sharp rap on the back door. But instead of Nigel it was Harriet Willoughby who stepped through the door.

"Well," Constance began nervously, "this is a surprise."

Harriet stopped in the doorway and stood with her hands clasped behind her back. Though she was dressed in her usual boy's clothes, her hair had been neatly combed into a long pigtail, and her face was clean. At her heels, Alexander had been brushed until each separate hair shone, and there was actually a bit of ribbon tied around his neck.

In an uncharacteristically low voice Harriet addressed Elisande. "We come to thank you, me and Halexander. Warn't for you, 'e could've been drownded by them barstids."

Constance looked alarmed as Harriet whipped out a hand from behind her back, but there was only a nosegay of wildflowers in the girl's small fist. She held them out to Elisande saying in the same uncertain tone, "These is fer you."

Surprised and touched, Elisande accepted the little bouquet. The flowers had been selected and arranged with great care even though the stems had been mashed by being held too tightly in Harriet's nervous hand.

"These are lovely," she exclaimed. "I recognize wild aster and marigold and goldenrod but not these others. Do you know their names, Con?"

Eagerly Constance walked over to examine the little nosegay. "Why, here is lovage and herb Robert, and spikenard, too. *Wherever* did you get such lovely lovage? I have been searching for some for the longest time."

She beamed upon Harriet who said with unaccustomed shyness, "Them herbs grow down by the old mill, behind the fence. Nobody knows where, but me. I'll bring yer some more, if yer want."

"Or perhaps you could show me where they grow?" Constance asked hopefully. "Tea made with lovage is very good for the throat."

"Guess I could an' all—" but Harriet's voice

trailed off as the front door swung open and Nigel strode in.

"Lisa," he began, "it's time to go."

He stopped short as his eyes fell on Alexander, who was sitting in the middle of the hearth rug. "What's that damned beast doing here?" Nigel exploded.

"Yer keep yer mitts off Halexander, yer great lummox," Harriet screeched. She snatched up her dog, stuck out her tongue at Nigel, and slammed the door.

Constance looked distressed. "There was no need to *shout*, Nigel," she reproved. "Harriet and I were having a conversation."

Nigel glowered at the closed door but only asked, "Are you ready to ride, Lisa?"

Leaving Constance to pore over Harriet's floral offering, Elisande followed Nigel outdoors where Parse was holding the horses' reins. His lumpy countenance had been twisted into an expression of deep gloom and apprehension, and he kept glancing over his shoulder.

"What ails Parse?" Elisande wondered as she and Nigel left the village for the common road. "Did something happen during your ride this morning?"

"What?" Nigel asked in a distracted voice. "No— not that I know of. Saw nothing and met nobody except the widow Willoughby who asked Parse if he could move a heavy chest for her." He broke off, chewed his bottom lip for a fierce moment, and then exclaimed, "Hell and the devil, Lisa. I don't know if I can go through with this."

Her own doubts were making her impatient. "Why not?" Elisande demanded.

"Sylvia might be feeling sorry for me. Don't want her pity, by God."

"Then don't pity yourself," Elisande flared. After

a moment she added in a quieter tone, "I'm sorry, but you must believe in yourself if others are to believe in you."

Unexpectedly Nigel broke into a wan smile. "Deserved that. Been the devil to live with, lately. But, Lisa—you have no idea what it is to live inside my skin. For all I know, I might have sold those papers to the Frogs."

"I don't believe it for a second," Elisande retorted with spirit. "You are a gallant and loyal gentleman. You were trusted by the colonel and your advancement was assured. Why would you have turned traitor?"

"Because I was poor and wanted to marry Miss Hanard," Nigel replied bluntly. "For Sylvia's sake I'd have sold my soul to the devil."

"Your soul, maybe, but not your country. That you could never do, Nigel. I would stake my life on that."

The conviction in her voice finally pierced his gloom. Elisande saw the tense, brittle lines of her brother's face smooth slowly out. He closed his eyes and drew in a long breath that was almost a sigh.

"What a good soldier you are," he murmured huskily. "And what a self-pitying, sniveling beast I am. Ah, Lisa. Without you and Con I'd have been finished a long time ago."

Tears gritted her eyelids. As she reached out her hand to him, Elisande was reminded of the time when she was seven and Nigel three. They had slipped out of the house at night and played in the woods but then hadn't been able to find their way back to the house. Nigel had been terrified, but he had been so brave. He had held tight to her hand and never made a sound.

He was holding tightly now. "Thank you for your handsome praise, sir, but you must give over speaking foolishness," she said as lightly as she

we must be going. Sylvia, if you don't return to Hanard House at once, your father might become suspicious."

"Pooh, we're safe enough," Sylvia laughed. She was in high curl, and her eyes shone like stars. "Stepmama has it all in hand. She has badgered Papa into going with her to show the garden and the Cliff Path to one of her gaming friends—a thoroughly odious griffin, I might add. They were waiting for her to come to Hanard House when I left."

Elisande's heart sank further. "Not Lady Carme?"

"How did you know?" Sylvia pulled her lovely features into an imitation of Lady Carme's malicious scowl. "What a muffin-faced squeeze-crab she is, Elisande. She protests that she's stepmama's bosom bow—but I collect that's because Anabelle loses so much to her at piquet and faro. Stepmama is making the Carme woman rich."

She would have rattled on, but Elisande stopped her. "I saw Lady Carme's carriage pass by ten minutes ago. I fear she recognized me—and you, too, Sylvia."

Nigel said worriedly, "I'll ride back to Hanard House with you, Sylvia. Can't have you face your father alone."

"Better alone than with you," Elisande objected. "We should go our separate ways now." But Nigel insisted on escorting his lady at least to the fork in the road.

Sylvia agreed. "It is hard to say good-bye. Don't look so down pin, Elisande. Even if she has wings on her heels, Lady Carme won't reach Hanard House for another ten minutes."

But as they rounded the curve in the road that led to the fork, there was the sound of galloping hoofbeats. Nigel swore beneath his breath.

"The colonel," he gritted. "Lisa, take Sylvia and

ride back the way we came till you reach Swan's Cove. Then follow the smugglers' road through the woods to Hanard House. Sylvia knows the way."

But Sylvia tossed her head and declared she was not about to abandon her Nigel. "Anyway," she added, "Papa has seen us."

The colonel, cloak flying and graying head bare to the wind, was riding toward them like a man possessed. Elisande's heart sank to her boots, but Sylvia tossed her head and called, "Papa—what are you doing out here?"

"What an *I* doing here?" The colonel repeated. He was so angry and shocked that he could hardly speak. "What are *you* doing here, you minx? Eh? You were supposed never to leave your room without permission and here you are without even a groom attending you."

Once more Sylvia tossed her fiery curls. "I had the headache, so I slipped out to get some exercise. What is wrong with that? Sound body, sound mind, as you are always preaching at me. And while I was riding, I met Miss Redding and her brother. It was purest chance."

The colonel squared around to face Nigel. "*Was* it chance?" he barked. "Eh?"

Color rushed to Nigel's cheeks. His mouth hardened, and he drew himself up in the saddle. "Won't lie about it to you, sir. No. But," he added hastily, "my sister acted as chaperon. The proprieties—"

"To hell with the proprieties," fumed the colonel. "I gave orders that there was to be no more of these meetings between the two of you. Now I see that my commands mean nothing. Eh? Next time I find you within ten miles of my daughter, I'll thrash you like the cur you are."

Elisande saw the angry flash in her brother's eyes and was terrified. If the colonel goaded Nigel into a duel, there would be hell itself to pay.

Determinedly she wedged her gelding between the two men. "There is no need for such outrageous talk, Colonel," she said sternly. "Nothing has happened today that can cause harm to anyone. You insult Miss Hanard as well as my brother by implying otherwise."

"Nothing? You call the seduction of a pure young girl by a damned traitor 'nothing'?" the colonel snarled.

Nigel opened his mouth to speak, but once more Elisande intervened. "There has been no seduction. Besides, you have no proof that my brother has done anything dishonorable. Your own military court exonerated him." She paused to add angrily, "How *dare* you speak of Nigel this way?"

"Yes," Sylvia echoed, "how dare you, Papa?" Her lip curled as she added, "If I recall, you *lied* to me about Nigel's letters. How can you accuse anybody of dishonor, especially without proof?"

"But I do have proof," the colonel grated.

"What proof? No," Nigel added sternly as Elisande began to speak again. "I want to hear this. What proof do you have, Colonel?"

In the sudden silence that fell upon them, Elisande could hear autumn insects busy in the underbrush. A thrush was trilling, and a cool wind soughed through the trees carrying with it the scent of new-mown hay from the farms down the road.

Against these innocent, familiar scents and sounds, Nigel's voice sounded harsh. "Let's hear your proof, Colonel."

"If it's not another of your lies, Papa," Sylvia added scornfully.

The colonel glowered at her then turned his gaze on Nigel. "The fact of the matter is that I saw you that night, Redding. Do you understand? I *saw* you coming out of my study where the military dispatches were kept."

"But Nigel was your aide. He was always in and out of your study," Sylvia interrupted indignantly. The colonel gestured her quiet.

"I saw you come out of the study," he repeated. "Eh? You stared up and down the hall as if you were afraid of being seen. Then, before I could call out to you, you ran down that hall as if the devil himself was hot on your heels. When I went into the study, I saw that the painting of Hercules had been pushed aside and that the wall safe stood open. The dispatches from Wellington were gone."

"No," Nigel whispered. *"No."*

"They were gone because you had stolen them," the colonel went on pitilessly. "Obviously, you didn't have time to cover your tracks. Eh? I must have surprised you in the very commission of your crime. That's why you ran."

Sylvia had turned very pale. "But," she faltered, "perhaps someone *else* took the dispatches. Yes—that must have been it."

"No one but Redding knew where I kept the spare key to the strongbox. No one else knew but my 'trusted' aide!"

Nigel's lips moved soundlessly in denial. Sylvia was staring at her father in mute horror. Elisande whispered, "But—but why did you not tell the military tribunal what you just told us? You said nothing about this."

"I didn't want my daughter's name dragged through the mud," Colonel Hanard replied wearily. "Eh? It'd have come out that Redding was infatuated with her. There'd have been talk that it was for her sake that he turned traitor. I didn't want Sylvia to become a seven-day wonder."

He paused, and then added sternly, "But I *know* what you did, Redding. You are a vile traitor who sold his country for money. If you truly have lost your memory, I feel sorry because you'll never know the depth of your perfidy. But memory or no memory, you are as guilty as Cain, and if I ever catch you near my daughter again, I'll shoot you."

He grasped hold of Sylvia's bridle and tugged it. The mare trotted obediently forward, with Sylvia sitting in the saddle as though stunned. She did not speak or protest or look back.

"On my life—she *believes* him." Elisande tore her eyes away from the colonel and saw that Nigel was staring after Sylvia as might a condemned man. "Oh, God, if I did what he said, I don't deserve to live."

He sawed his horse's head around and began to ride like a madman down the road. Elisande called out to him, but he did not turn. She started to follow him, then stopped and simply watched him go. There was nothing she could say or do that could possibly help.

"He'll come home when he's worn himself out," she told herself.

And prayed that she was right.

Morning lengthened into afternoon and then into the long English gloaming, but Nigel did not come home. Parse went looking for him and, tense and anxious, Elisande and Constance could do little but wait. They both ran to the door when they heard hoofbeats, but Parse was alone.

"I looked for him everywhere," the big Yorkshireman reported. "I called in at t'Gilded Stag, hoping that Lord Raven might be with t'captain, but t'marquess's valet—a mawworm as talked through his nose—said that neither his master nor Lord Raven were at home. He wunnot tell me where they went."

His worried eyes met Elisande's. "Nay, I came

back only t'see if he'd come home. I'st be going out again, and I'll find him. P'rhaps he's only stopped somewhere on t'road for a pint."

Or perhaps he has harmed himself. Elisande read her fear in Parse's eyes and spoke with an effort. "You must not go out again before you rest. You are tired and hungry and might miss something critical."

"But t'captain needs me!" Parse cried. "I'st all right, Miss Lisa."

"While Constance feeds you, I will ride back toward the Norman Church," Elisande went on doggedly.

The church was where Nigel had trysted with Sylvia Hanard. It was there that he would go to think or to—hastily, Elisande slammed her mind shut to that thought.

Ignoring Parse's arguments that it was too dark for anyone, especially a lady, to be abroad alone, that there were footpads abroad in the woods, and that the seashore at night was an eerie place where a man could almost believe in hobgoblins and flayboggarts, she pulled on her cloak and gave Constance a hug.

"I will be back soon," she promised.

The gelding was tethered outside the cottage. He threw up his head and *whuffed* out a greeting as Elisande came up, and she stroked him and apologized for riding him again tonight.

"When we find Nigel you will have oats and a good rest," she told it. "Now we must ride."

It was not dark, but a strong wind had sprung up so that Elisande was glad she had worn her winter cloak. The cloak belled about her as she trotted through the quiet village and then cantered past the fork in the road toward the Norman Church. There was no sign of her brother anywhere.

"Nigel," she called, but the wind sent back her voice and except for that echo, the dark woods were silent. She rode on and found the church, gray and shadowed in the gloaming and as deserted as the woods. When she called out, more echoes answered her.

Dismounting, Elisande searched the grounds of the church. Nothing. She walked through the surrounding woods. No one. In an attempt to keep her rising fear at bay, she told herself that her brother was a brave man who would not take the coward's way out. But when she thought of his face as she had last seen it, she could not believe her own words.

I don't deserve to live—

Hanard's voice had carried conviction this morning, and Nigel believed what the colonel had said. "He is wrong," Lisa told herself fiercely. "Perhaps Nigel surprised the thief who was taking the documents. Perhaps he was giving pursuit. That must have been what happened."

But, her common sense argued, if this were the case *why* had Nigel not given the alarm, or at least told someone about the theft? Why had he gone running down the corridor as if he had done something shameful?

An owl hooted from the abbey, and the lonely sound touched Elisande with a terrible sense of foreboding. For a moment, she felt despair. Then she remembered a deep voice saying, "There is always a way."

"Lord Raven," Elisande exclaimed aloud.

If only Lord Raven were here, he would know what to do. Of all the people she knew, he was the only man who could take command of this terrible situation.

Above the wind she could hear the sound of the sea, and that distant muttering reminded her of the day she had sailed with him at Swan's Cove. Parse had already looked along the shore, but perhaps he had missed something. Swan's Cove was where Nigel had been found on March thirtieth. Perhaps he was there now.

Remounting her horse, Elisande galloped toward the dunes. The way was familiar, but this ride was far different from the one she had taken with Lord Raven. Under the newly risen moon, the dunes had an eerie, almost haunted appearance. When something rustled amongst the furze, Elisande started.

Tales of footpads and outlaws that she had heard filled her mind, and for a moment she was afraid. Then a rabbit darted out of the underbrush. "I am as bad as Parse with his hobgoblins and flayboggarts," Elisande rallied herself.

She guided her horse onto the path between the dunes. About to urge her horse forward onto the beach, Elisande stopped as the moon swung from behind the clouds and illumined the sea.

"A schooner," Elisande exclaimed.

She could easily recognize the type of ship from the books she had read. The vessel was not very large, but it had clean, slim lines and a low, raking hull that had obviously been built for speed. With the moonlight dancing over its sails and its high spars, it looked proud and incredibly beautiful as it sailed toward the pier.

What would a schooner be doing sailing into Swan's Cove at such an hour? And why here rather than at one of the other, better-known docks or piers? As the question touched her mind, Elisande saw the flash of light and saw that two men were standing on the pier. One had a lamp with which he was signaling the approaching schooner.

Elisande recalled what Lord Raven had said about smugglers using the cove. Perhaps the "brethren of the coast" were still active—but before she could pursue this thought there was a hail from the schooner.

"Ahoy the shore," a man called. "Is that you, mi-lord?"

To Elisande's complete astonishment, a familiar voice made reply. "A good voyage, Mr. Follings?"

Lord Raven—and this stately vessel must therefore be the *Silver Raven*. As Elisande raised herself in her stirrups to see better, the man at the ship's rail was calling, "Aye, sir, it was indeed. And we have the precious cargo aboard, all safe and sound. Will it please you come aboard?"

"Precious cargo," Elisande repeated incredulously. Could Lord Raven be *smuggling*? She watched with growing unease as the schooner drew up to the pier and set anchor.

Lord Raven seemed in a hurry to board his schooner. Hardly was the gangplank down but he strode up onto the deck where he was greeted by two men. "No, not a man," Elisande exclaimed aloud. "It's a woman."

The woman who was coming forward to greet Lord Raven was tall and dressed in a light-colored hat and cloak that caught the shimmer of the ship's lamps. Elisande could not make out the woman's face, but she guessed that the lady in white was young and beautiful. She held herself proudly, and when Lord Raven swept off his hat and bowed over her hand, she seemed to accept the homage as her due.

With obvious pleasure, Lord Raven escorted the lady down onto the gangplank and onto the pier. Elisande felt an inexplicable tightening within her as she watched how his lordship's fair head bent low as he hung on the lady's every word. She looked back at the *Silver Raven* and noted that sailors were carrying down a steady stream of baggage. Apparently the lady in white had come to stay.

The sound of hoofbeats muffled by sand awakened her to the fact that Lord Raven's groom was leading forward his lordship's curricle. Elisande was angry with herself. What was she doing here, spying on Lord Raven and his amours? Nigel was not here. She must leave and find him. She must go *now*.

But as Elisande turned her horse, the wind changed and carried a snatch of conversation toward her. "It's good to see you," Elisande heard Lord Raven say. "I hardly dared hope you would answer my letter so quickly. It matters a great deal to me that you have come."

His deep voice was sincere, almost ardent. In response came a rich contralto. "Why, she is speaking in French," Elisande exclaimed.

Lord Raven answered in the same language. Elisande strained her ears to try and follow the conversation, but they were either speaking in lower voices, or the fickle wind had changed direction. All she could catch were a few words here and there that made no sense. But since when had love talk ever made sense?

Anabelle Hanard had warned her not to trust Lord Raven. She had hinted that he was a man of the world with many broken hearts to his discredit.

Elisande reminded herself of Anabelle Hanard's words as she hastily urged her horse back between the dunes. Forewarned was forearmed. Yet, all the same, she could not help remembering Lord Raven's promise that he would one day take her to sea on the *Silver Raven*.

"He and his 'precious cargo' can do as they like," she muttered under her breath. "*I* must find Nigel."

Chapter Eight

Constance was waiting at the door when Elisande at last returned to Willoughby Cottage. "Has he come home yet?" Elisande called.

Mournfully her cousin shook her head. "Parse went out again as soon as he had eaten," she reported. "He said he could not sit by and do nothing."

"I must see to this poor horse." Wearily Elisande dismounted and then burst out, "Oh, Con, I went everywhere I could think of, but I couldn't find him. I don't know where else to look."

Constance looked ready to cry. But when Elisande came in after rubbing down and feeding the gelding, she found her cousin busy making toast whilst a teakettle whistled merrily on the hob. "You must be cold after your long ride," Constance said. "And I am persuaded Nigel will be hungry when he returns home."

Elisande sank gratefully into a chair and watched the firelight burnish Constance's absorbed countenance. After all the anxieties and frustrations of the day and night, it was wonderfully reassuring to see her bustling about and preparing tea.

"It makes one hope there may be a tomorrow after all," she mused.

Constance did not ask what Elisande meant. "This will refresh you," she said offering a cup of fragrant liquid. "That child, Harriet, came back shortly after you left this morning and we walked together to collect some herbs and even some wild honey! We had such a pleasant talk and—Elisande, can you credit it? Harriet cannot read or write."

Constance shook her head over the enormity of this. "She insists that she is too stupid to learn, but—listen! do you hear *hoofbeats*?"

They flew to the small window together in time to see a rider canter up to the cottage door. "Thank God," Elisande breathed as she recognized Nigel's slender form with Parse riding pillion. "Thank God he is safe." She and Constance hugged each other, and Elisande cautioned, "We mustn't ask him any questions—not tonight."

Brittle and white but determined to act as if nothing was wrong, Nigel sauntered into the cottage. He volunteered no information as to where he had been and made a jest of the fact that Parse had run him to ground at the Gilded Stag. "Stopped to speak to Raven, but he was away," he explained. "Lord, but it's cold out tonight. Good thing you girls stopped at home."

He drank two cups of Constance's tea and ate half a loaf's worth of toast before going to bed. Parse then led the horses away to be stabled at the inn, and the small household finally settled down to rest.

Worn out from the long vigil, Constance fell asleep almost at once, but Elisande lay wide awake. Interwoven with her fears for her brother were memories of Lord Raven and his "precious cargo." No wonder the man had not returned to the inn.

"He must have sent his schooner to fetch *her* from France," Elisande muttered aloud into the darkness. "No doubt he was so bored that he needed some more 'distraction.' "

Determinedly Elisande dismissed thoughts of his

lordship. What Lord Raven did or did not do did not signify. What mattered was Nigel, and so tomorrow they must return to Sussex. Nothing more was to be gained by staying in Dorset, and none of them could live through another night like this one.

She made her announcement next morning at breakfast. Constance clapped her hands, and Parse's lumpy face creased in a wide grin. "Eh, but that's good hearing, ma'am," he exclaimed. "I can get us packed faster than a flea's leap."

"Don't blame any of you for going back." They all turned to Nigel who, gaunt and red eyed, was cradling a cup of tea in his hands. "But I can't leave. Not yet."

He swung to his feet and began to pace about the room. "I need to go back to Hanard House," he finally said.

"Nigel, the colonel said he'd shoot you!"

"Impossible! The cards say that the way is full of danger."

Both women had spoken at once. Nigel turned to give them a pale smile. "Do you think I care?"

"But *we* care," Constance pointed out in her gruffest voice. "We care very much indeed."

Parse said nothing but cast an anxious look at his employer, who said, "I dreamed again last night. First, I dreamed of books. *Open* books. Then I saw that woman again."

"The lady with the Spanish combs?" Elisande asked quickly.

Nigel nodded. "Saw her walking in the Hanards' garden. She was going along the Cliff Path, and there was something familiar—and frightening—about her." He paused to add earnestly, "I'm remembering more and more. Have a notion that soon I'll remember it all."

Constance looked frightened. Elisande forced herself to ask calmly, "What do you plan to do?"

"One way or another, I have to find out if the colonel's right about me. You were right about one thing, Lisa—the answers are at Hanard House. Have to go back tonight."

Parse immediately said, "I'll go wi' tha, Captain."

A sweet smile touched Nigel's pale lips. His eyes softened, and the tormented, wild look left them for a moment. "No, old friend," he said gently. "Not this time. No," he added more sternly, as Parse began to argue. "I need you to take care of the ladies and get them safely back to Sussex if—that's an order."

Parse snapped to attention so violently that the crockery rattled. Knowing that there was no use protesting, Elisande said, "Why run the risk of meeting the colonel? I will send word to Anabelle and ask her to find a time when you can go safely."

"And who'd take the message to her?" Nigel demanded. "The colonel'd recognize Parse and intercept a note, and after yesterday you and Con would be *persona non grata.*"

"Perhaps Lord Raven would carry the message," Constance suggested.

"No," Elisande said sharply. "We have bothered his lordship enough. This is something we must do for ourselves."

Just then, there was a muffled bark on the street outside and a child's high voice. "Harriet," Elisande exclaimed. "How perfect. The colonel would never suspect a child."

"Gone soft in the head, Lisa? As if we could trust that brat," Nigel snapped, but Constance came to the rescue.

"Lisa is right. I am persuaded that the child can be trusted to keep her silence. Besides, there is no one else."

Elisande called to Harriet, who came trotting into the cottage. She glanced at Nigel askance while Elisande explained the situation, then agreed to carry a note to Mrs. Hanard. "Nobody else'll get 'is mitts on it," she vowed, "else Halexander will bite 'im."

Alexander, who was sitting at Constance's feet, lifted his lip and growled at Nigel. Diplomatically suggesting that the dog should wait outside, Elisande sat down to compose a message to the colonel's wife. "And when you return," Constance added, "come back and have some tea with me. You will see what I have done with the herbs we gathered yesterday."

After Harriet had gone, Nigel professed himself too nervous to remain at home and, with Parse in close attendance, strode away on a walk. "It's better for him to be doing something," Elisande said as she carried some mending with her and went to darn by the light of the small window. "Don't worry so much, Con. Parse is with him."

"I was thinking of Harriet, not Nigel," Constance confessed. She picked up a book on herbs that lay open on the table and shook her head over it. "Imagine not being able to read."

"Many children cannot read. Their families are too poor and need them at home to work. It's a sad shame, but that is life. Besides, many so-called educated people do not care to read."

"It is because they are not exposed to the proper books," Constance said earnestly. "Take the marquess, for instance. He had no interest in reading until I showed him Burlow's book on *Bees and Their Apiaries*."

Noting the gleam of satisfaction in her cousin's small brown eyes, Elisande could not help smiling. "I collect that the marquess found the book as fascinating as the lady who introduced him to it."

"As the—oh, you are funning me." Constance flushed a little, chuckled, then added, "But he did beg to borrow the book from me. You see? It is a matter of stimulating the interest!"

Harriet did not return for several hours. "I 'ad to wait until Mrs. 'Anard were alone, like you said," she explained when she finally reappeared. "T'colonel was with 'is missus for the longest time."

She handed a note to Elisande, who read it quickly. "Thank the Lord for Anabelle Hanard," she exclaimed. Then, seeing Nigel and Parse walking back toward the cottage she added, "And thank you, Harriet. I don't know how we could have managed without you."

Leaving Constance to give Harriet the promised tea, she went outside to greet Nigel and give him the note. "I told you that she'd help us," she said. "If we go tonight at nine o'clock, she says the colonel will not be there."

Nigel arched his brows. "*We*, sister?"

Elisande pretended not to hear. "Anabelle says that she will meet us in the garden and will keep watch while you wander through the garden and the house. So will I."

"I'm going alone, Lisa."

Hot protests rushed to her lips, but she forced them back. "As you wish."

"I don't mean to sound ungrateful." Nigel put an arm around her shoulders as he added, "You're the best sister a man ever had. Told Raven so today when I met him."

She refused to acknowledge the quickening of her heart. "Indeed," she said coolly.

"Parse and I met him near the inn," Nigel explained. "He sent his compliments and said he'd be calling on you soon."

"Will he so?" Elisande murmured and could not keep from asking, "What was Lord Raven doing this morning?"

"What? Oh—driving a female around in his curricle," Nigel replied in a preoccupied tone.

He began to care for his horse, and Elisande could hear him whistling softly as he worked. Strangers would have thought he had not a care in the world, but Parse would have recognized the set look in his eyes. Nigel was hazarding his life and happiness on a throw of the dice, and devil take the cost.

Mired in gloom, Elisande returned to the house where she found Constance laying out her tarot cards. Harriet, big eyed, stood at her elbow.

"I am teaching Harriet to read," Constance explained happily.

"Using the *tarot*?"

Constance nodded and pointed to one of the cards. "Here is a happy card meaning hope and trust, Harriet. Can you find the *a* in the Star card?"

Hope and trust—with an ache of the heart, Elisande turned away. She herself was to blame for actually allowing herself to trust Lord Raven. Because of him, she had almost allowed herself to hope that things would work out for Nigel and for the Reddings as well.

But now that futile hope was gone, and she must deal with reality. Elisande went in search of Parse, who was stacking wood outside the kitchen. When she told him what she wanted, an expression of profound anxiety furrowed his broad countenance. "I cannot do that, ma'am," he exclaimed. "T'captain'd never forgive me."

"He won't take you with him, and you know I cannot let him go alone. I need the gelding saddled and waiting, Parse. I must follow him before he gets too much of a head start." Then, as the big Yorkshireman still hesitated she added urgently, "*If* something goes wrong, I must be there."

Parse spoke bluntly. "Eh, ma'am, it won't do.

Should he try t'put a bullet in his brain, tha'll not be strong enough to stop him."

She had thought of that, too. Her throat tightened, but she managed to say quite calmly, "If I am there with him, he will hold his hand. Anyway, it's a risk I must take."

Parse sighed. "Aye, well—I'll saddle up t'horse. Lord Raven wouldn't be going along with tha?" he added hopefully. "It's be that much safer."

"Lord Raven," Elisande said dryly, "has his own concerns to keep him busy."

That night, Elisande watched her brother eat cabbage and mutton broth with a good appetite, and then put on his coat and put his pistol in his belt. After he had kissed her and Constance and ridden off, Elisande hurried to put on her cloak.

"You are following Nigel, are you not?" Constance asked. When Elisande nodded, she added, "I wish I could offer some help, but—oh, it is most provoking."

She broke off and stared in exasperation at the cards spread out in front of her. "Come and look at this, Elisande."

Outside, Elisande could hear Nigel talking to Parse. "I haven't the time," she said, trying to mask her impatience. "What is the matter, Con?"

"The cards are the matter. When I was teaching Harriet to read, they kept falling in the same way, over and over." Constance rubbed the bridge of her nose and glared at the cards. "They are telling us whether or not Nigel will remember what happened on March thirtieth."

In spite of her skepticism, Elisande felt a surge both of hope and fear. "And will he remember?"

"I do not know," Constance said crossly. "The nearest I could get out of the cards is 'yes,' and then again, 'no.' " She held up a card of a man balancing two pentacles. "See? I just laid them out again and here is the Two of Pentacles once more."

Hoofbeats pounded outside. Elisande hurried out of doors to where Parse was waiting with the saddled gelding. "Be careful," he warned tersely as he helped her up. "Luck ride wi' thee."

Setting spurs to the horse, Elisande rode after Nigel. Close enough to keep him in sight, far enough to keep from being observed, she followed him down the road that led past the village toward Hanard House. There was a cutting wind, and the cloudy night was dark. The road to Hanard House had never seemed so long before, and it seemed to take forever to reach the fork in the road. As she rode, Elisande recalled Constance's cards and their prediction.

"It is superstitious nonsense," she told herself stoutly. "Lord Raven is right."

Elisande wished that she had not thought of Lord Raven. Her thoughts conjured up the man, self-assured, strong, and competent. If only he were riding with her now—"But he isn't," Elisande said aloud, causing the gelding to snort and toss his head. "I must stop chasing rainbows, and—ah, here is the fork in the road at last."

As she spoke, she heard a rustling in the woods by the side of the road. Turning her head, Elisande saw a dark shadow emerging from the trees.

She had barely time to cry out before someone lunged forward and seized the bridle of her horse. Taken by surprise, the gelding whinnied its distress and reared up on its haunches.

"Let go of my bridle!" Elisande slashed at her attacker with her riding crop, and he cursed and let her go. As she fought to control the plunging gelding, she saw other shadows further on down the road.

"Nigel!" she screamed. "Behind you, Nigel! 'Ware your back!"

She could not tell whether he had heard because her terrified horse pawed air, almost throwing her from the saddle. "Bloody bitch," a rough voice raged. "Get orf that 'orse, damn yer."

Rough hands seized her legs and commenced dragging her from the saddle. She beat him with her crop, but to no avail. Fighting and clawing, she was dragged down from the saddle and flung roughly on the ground.

There was the drum of horses' hooves nearby. Nigel was coming to her rescue. Elisande scrambled to her feet crying, "Be careful, Nigel—"

Her words were cut off by a blow that knocked her sprawling again, and a flat, vicious, unpleasantly familiar face pushed itself close to hers. Too well Elisande remembered Mingus, one of the ruffians involved in trying to drown Harriet's dog. When she saw the knife in the man's hand, she kicked out at him with all her strength.

"Izzat all you can do, missy?" the man sneered. "C'mon, then, fight fer yer life. Beg me ter spare yer. Makes it more fun, see."

He taunted her with his knife. Elisande tried once more to regain her feet, but he guffawed and pinned her down. The knife arced up, and as if from far away, she heard herself call out a name.

Almost simultaneously there was a scream. Elisande thought that it had been her own, but next moment, her attacker fell heavily beside her. She screamed in good earnest as strong arms caught her and dragged her to her feet.

"Be still—you're safe," Lord Raven's harsh voice said. "Did that bastard hurt you?"

He turned her around to face him as he spoke, and she managed to gasp, "They're attacking Nigel—"

As if in answer, she heard her brother's triumphant yell rising over a babble of shouts and curses. "Not so fast, you damned villain—not finished with you yet," Nigel was shouting.

Nigel was apparently very much alive. She wanted to go to him, but when she tried to move, the world turned upside down, and Elisande was forced to cling to Lord Raven for support.

He held her close against him, and she felt his hand stroking back her hair. "Easy," he was saying in a husky voice that she could hardly recognize as belonging to his lordship. "Be easy, now. It's over, and I have you safe."

She knew she should move, but all strength seemed to have left her. Her limbs felt useless, and when she moved her head, she felt sick and dizzy again. "Hush," Lord Raven said. "Be quiet for a moment, and the world will right itself."

"Nigel needs help—"

"Why spoil his fun? He's got the hedge-rats on the run, and he's enjoying himself." Lord Raven's voice was soothing. It gentled the fear of what had almost happened, blunted the nightmare of Mingus and his knife. "Anyway, my groom has gone to his assistance."

Fun—she shivered as she managed to ask. "Where did you come from?"

"My groom saw Nigel ride past the Gilded Stag," he explained. "When you followed a few minutes later, he knew there'd be trouble, so he told me."

And it was a good thing that Perkins had done so, Lord Raven thought. He could feel Elisande shuddering in his arms, and those bone-deep tremors caused a wave of rage at her attackers. Mingled with this anger was the inexpressible feeling of thanksgiving that she was unhurt. Lord Raven, who had never set foot in a church save for funerals and had not so much as uttered a prayer since his early boyhood, sent up a fervent testimonial to Whoever was listening. *Thank You for letting me be near enough to help her.*

She was so slender in his arms, nestled there as if she had been made to fit against him. An ache to kiss the tremor from her soft lips filled him, and with that an almost unbearable tenderness. No longer did Lord Raven bother to remind himself of the consequences of such feelings. He already knew the consequences.

"Fate," he said resignedly.

She looked up at the word. His lordship was holding her closely. As closely perhaps, as he had held the French lady in white.

Ignoring a lingering dizziness, Elisande placed her palms flat against his lordship's hard chest and pushed herself backward out of his arms. "I am all right," she said firmly. "Please, will you help Nigel?"

"Lisa—Lisa, I heard you call. Are you all right?"

Nigel had ridden up. He was hatless, and the night wind ruffled his fair hair as he swung down from his horse to demand, "Those scoundrels didn't hurt you, did they? Thank God you were by, Raven—even though your man did spoil my sport."

"No harm has come to your sister," Lord Raven said. He was not sure whether he was glad or sorry that Nigel had ridden up when he did.

"But they have hurt *you*," Elisande cried. "You're bleeding, Nigel!"

Her brother raised his hand to his cheek. "Scratch, Lisa, I assure you," he said cheerfully. "What are you doing here, anyway? Thought I told you—"

He broke off as he saw Mingus lying on the grass. In a very different voice he asked, "Is he dead?"

Lord Raven turned over the body with the toe of

his boot. "We won't be able to question this fellow. Unfortunately, I was in a hurry at the time. Did you take any prisoners, Nigel?"

"Winged one and hit another," Nigel reported grimly. "There were five of them, as far as I could tell. The bas—scoundrels melted back into the woods, and I was too worried about Lisa to follow, so no one's left to interrogate. What's to be done?"

"There might be more of them about. We must get your sister back to safety, so you might as well abandon your idea of riding out to Hanard House for tonight." Lord Raven smiled at the younger man's astonishment. "Where else would you be going hell and be damned at this time of the night?"

Leaving Lord Raven's groom to report the attack to the proper authorities, the others rode back toward the village. Nigel's wound was less superficial than he had claimed, for even with Lord Raven's handkerchief tied around his forehead, blood had seeped through the cloth by the time they approached the village. On the outskirts they found Parse on foot, hurrying toward Hanard House.

"Nay, tha didn't say as I couldn't follow on Shank's Mare," he exclaimed when he saw them. Then his belligerence melted and he smote his thighs with both fists. "Oh, Captain sir, tha'rt wounded. I knew I should've gone along with tha no matter what tha said."

As he grasped Nigel's bridle and urged the horse forward, Lord Raven asked Elisande, "What exactly happened at the rendezvous yesterday?"

Elisande told him, adding, "That is why Nigel felt he had to return to Hanard House tonight. He hoped that there he would finally remember everything."

As she spoke, he watched how the lamplight from the approaching cottage fell on her white face. So lovely she was, with courage twice any man's, and a spirit that he had admired from the first. But, Raven wondered, did she have the courage to do as he proposed?

She was saying, "I have not thanked you for saving my life." He gestured away her thanks, but she went on earnestly, "And very likely you saved Nigel's life, too. Those thieves would have killed us both if they could."

"You're sure they were footpads, then?"

"What else could they have been?"

"I wonder," Lord Raven said softly.

They had reached Willoughby Cottage, and he halted his horse, swung down, and walked around to her. But instead of helping her down, Lord Raven reached up to take her hands and hold them in a tight grip. "Do you dare find out the truth?" he asked. "Even if it may not be the truth you want?"

Elisande felt a shiver of ice crawl along her spine. "Do you know something?" she whispered. "If you do, I pray you tell me. Not knowing is worse than torture."

"*I* don't know, but there is a way if you are willing to follow that road."

He was looking up into her face, their hands tightly meshed together. She bent down until their faces were so close that stray curls of her hair fell against his cheek. "Yes," she was saying, "yes. We must know or we will go mad."

Her hair was fragrant. Her eyes were luminous in the lamplight, her mouth as soft as a flower. Raven felt something in his heart shift, tug loose of its moorings, and slide softly out to sea.

"Elisande," he said, "I—"

They were interrupted by a loud wail. Elisande pulled her hands free from Lord Raven's clasp as the cottage door opened to disclose Constance. "They have killed you, Nigel!" Constance wailed.

"Nonsense. Fit as a fiddle, Con. Don't squawk

about it," Nigel protested, but he staggered a little as he dismounted, and Parse ran to help him inside the cottage.

"*How* will we learn the truth?" Elisande asked urgently.

Without answering, Lord Raven helped her to dismount. Her heart had begun to pound with apprehension and the inescapable fact that being with Lord Raven affected her in ways she could not understand. Even after what she had seen at Swan's Cove, after what she knew about his Frenchwoman, it only took the man's hard grasp about her waist to bring back memories of a sunlit glade.

Elisande realized that my lord had asked her a question. "I beg your pardon?" she asked as steadily as she could.

"Have you heard of mesmerism?"

"I—I believe so. Con once told me about Mesmer—he was an Austrian, was he not?—who thought that he had the power of magnetic healing."

"Miss Dayton is well informed," Lord Raven said. "Mesmer called his healing force animal magnetism and had some success in healing hysterical patients. But he was thought to be a charlatan and his ideas fell into disrepute."

"I don't see what this has to do with Nigel," Elisande protested.

"Mesmer's ideas have been expanded and used by a gifted few. These 'mesmerists' are able to reach into a troubled mind and help. I told you that everything has a scientific explanation, didn't I?" Lord Raven paused to ask. "Well, I saw this entire episode with my own eyes."

Elisande listened, astounded, as Lord Raven related a story that had occurred in the south of France a year before. "A young girl was plagued with a recurring nightmare in which she was torn apart by savage wolves. It terrified her so much she couldn't sleep at all. Her frightened parents—friends of mine, by the way—consulted a score of physicians before calling in a well-known mesmerist, who put the girl into a light trance and helped her to retrace the events that had caused the nightmares."

"And did she remember?" Elisande hardly dared to ask.

Lord Raven nodded. "Apparently the child had been badly frightened by a neighbor's dog when she was still in leading strings. Her conscious mind buried the incident deep, but the subconscious memory remained. Once she remembered and confronted her fear, the girl never had another nightmare."

With some difficulty, Elisande swallowed the knot that had formed in her throat. "You think that this method would help Nigel." He nodded. "You think perhaps that his memory has been repressed and has burrowed deep."

Lord Raven shrugged. "It's worth a chance."

"But how would I apply to this mesmerist? Where would we have to go?"

He checked her stream of questions by saying, "There's no need to go anywhere. Mme Benoit is here in Dorset. I sent the *Silver Raven* to fetch her from Paris when I realized that her skills could help your brother. She landed here last evening."

The lady in white was a mesmerist. Lord Raven had sent his own schooner to fetch her to Dorset so that she could help Nigel. In spite of all her uncertainty, Elisande had the incredible feeling that a boulder had rolled away from her shoulders.

"Oh," she whispered. "That was so kind of you. But—but what will Nigel say?"

"That's a problem," Lord Raven admitted. "Mme

Benoit can't do anything to help your brother if he doesn't cooperate. And since he didn't see her in action, he'd be justified in believing that she was a simple trickster."

Lord Raven paused. "More to the point, do *you* believe?"

The golden light of the cottage lamp threw the hard lines of his features into bold relief, caught the light in his eyes. Once more she recalled Constance's cards. *Hope and faith*, she thought.

"I would not hurt you for the world," Lord Raven was saying. His voice was quiet, almost detached, but the expression in his eyes was anything but dispassionate. "I don't want to make things worse than they already are. Mme Benoit is here in Dorset if you require her services, but you must make the decision, Elisande."

The sound of her name on his lips caused her to catch her breath. Hearing that small, hushed sound, he looked more closely at her. Like stars, the lamplight was reflected in her eyes, and as he looked into them, she smiled tremulously.

Raven could no more resist that smile than he could fly. As if by their own volition, his arms closed about her, drawing her close. "Elisande," he whispered, as her lips lifted to his.

Once again Elisande felt the world slide away. The events of the night dissolved into a wondrous delirium. Warm shudders ran through her veins as she felt the passionate stroking of Lord Raven's mouth. The earth beneath her seemed to move, disintegrate, so that she had no support but his arms about her. Incredible sensations filled her, and she seemed to be lifted from the earth and rising toward the sky.

She wanted nothing more than to be here in his arms forever. Nothing mattered. Here there was no sorrow or loneliness or cold or dark. And there was no thought, too—except one. And that was that when Mingus was about to cut her throat, she had not screamed out for Nigel but for Ivo, Lord Raven.

He was murmuring her name as he kissed her, and Elisande willed herself to hear nothing but that sound. But now another thought was forming in her fogged mind. *She* might feel no sorrow or cold but Nigel did.

Her brother, Nigel. Nigel, who had been wounded tonight because his quest for memory had led them both into peril. At the thought of their danger, the beautiful world that had encapsulated Elisande shriveled away and she felt cold again.

Raven felt her grow tense in his arms and knew that Elisande was drawing away from him. For a moment he was tempted to kiss her again and still again until she forgot everything else save him— but this, he knew, was folly.

Reluctantly he loosened his arms around her. For a long moment they stood together in the cool darkness, and when he spoke his voice was studiedly matter-of-fact. "Shall I ask Mme Benoit to help your brother or send her back to France? Yes or no?"

The door of the cottage banged open and Nigel came out to call, "Lisa—Raven? What are you two doing out there whispering together?"

Elisande drew a deep, steadying breath, but even so her voice shook like a candle flame in the wind. "Lord Raven has been telling me about a Mme Benoit," she said. "He believes that she can help you remember, Nigel. And so do I."

Chapter Nine

"Can't think why I let you convince me to try this mesmerism gibberish."

" 'There are more things in heaven and earth,' Nigel. How can you dismiss something you have never tried as gibberish?"

Nigel and Constance eyed each other irritably across the fire in the narrow hearth. In spite of that cheerful fire and the pleasant arrangement of autumn flowers on the little tea table, the room was anything but comfortable. In fact, it crackled with tension.

"You agreed to let Mme Benoit help you," Elisande reminded her brother.

"Only because Raven took all the trouble to bring the woman from France. He'd saved your life, hadn't he? On my life, it would've been rag-mannered not to agree."

Elisande turned away from the fire, and Constance growled, "Now you have hurt Lisa's feelings."

Remorsefully Nigel strode across the room and hugged his sister. "I'm sorry," he muttered. "I don't know what I'm saying anymore."

She hugged him back. "My feelings are not hurt, really. I am only thinking."

Con added, "And I am sorry I snapped, Nigel. We are all as nervous as cats thinking about this mesmerist."

But Elisande had not been thinking solely of

Mme Benoit. Since Lord Raven had kissed her for the second time, Elisande had discovered that she could hardly put two thoughts together without his lordship appearing in them. Last night, when she had at last fallen into a troubled sleep, she had dreamed of him sailing on the *Silver Raven* with the woman in white.

She knew so little about Lord Raven. His adventures and experiences made the sum total of her existence seem incredibly dull. And yet, last night she had gone so eagerly into his arms—

There was the sound of hoofbeats outside, and Constance, who was nearest the window, announced, "Lord Raven has arrived."

Peering over the top of her cousin's head, Elisande could see that his lordship's curricle had indeed pulled up and that next to him was a tall, strikingly handsome lady. Her stylish hat of white-banded sarcenet was the perfect foil for a sleek, jet-black chignon. Her velvet pelisse was trimmed with ermine.

"Doesn't look like any mesmerist to me," Nigel muttered. Then he added impatiently as his eye fell on a stocky gentleman who was trotting his horse behind the curricle, "For the Lord's sake, there's Tanner come with them. Bad enough that I'm to do this thing. I won't have busy-heads listening."

He strode out of doors. Elisande followed in time to hear her brother demand, "Raven, what's your brother doing here? Thought this was to be a private affair."

Lord Raven cocked an eyebrow at his brother, who drew his brows together and attempted to stare haughtily down his nose. "Maybe the fellow's got somethin' to hide," he sneered.

"Was that to *my* address?" Nigel took a step forward, but Elisande caught his arm.

"Flying into the boughs will not help," she said. "But I, too, fail to see why the marquess is here."

Looking stubborn, the little marquess declared that he was there as a witness. "I have a stake in what comes of these proceedin's and insist on bein' here," he added.

Lord Raven said sternly, "Remember that you promised that you'd stay silent and out of the way if Madame consented to let you come."

"Maybe there won't be any mesmer—whatchumaycallit," growled the marquess. "All I'm saying is that maybe Redding has second thoughts about rememberin' what he did on March thirtieth. That is, if he ever forgot."

Nigel shrugged free of Elisande and took several steps toward his rival. But before he could speak, Mme Benoit intervened. Her voice was almost contralto and sounded a touch nasal, as if she were nursing a cold.

"*Alors*," she said calmly, "there is nothing to fear from what is to come, monsieur." She added to Nigel, "I will not force you to do anything that you yourself are unwilling to do. It may be that I can 'elp you break down the wall you 'ave built in your mind, but never will I impose my will on yours."

The marquess muttered something under his breath. Nigel frowned. Constance said anxiously, "We are all grateful you have come to help my cousin learn the truth, madame."

She cast a pleading look at the marquess, who flushed, looked suddenly embarrassed, and muttered, "Just so. Ah, just—ah, so. I say, what the deuce are we waitin' around for? Might as well get it over and done with."

Parse went to hold the marquess's horse as Lord Raven helped the French lady down from the curricle. She surveyed the small cottage critically before inclining her head in a regal nod. *"Eh, bien,"* she announced, "I am at your disposal."

Elisande led the way up the stairs and stood aside for the mesmerist. A fragrance of attar of roses mingled with sandalwood filled the air as Mme Benoit swept into the small room, surveyed it with one swift, keen look, and announced imperiously, "Mademoiselle, the fire gives too much light. I wish the room dark. Pray ring for the servants to close the curtains."

There were no curtains, so Elisande and Constance covered the small window with a blanket while Parse damped down the fire. Meanwhile, Madame removed her pelisse and Elisande noted that the lady had embellished her simple but fashionably cut dress of white jaconet muslin with ropes of jet-and-black pearls. Amongst these ebony strands flashed a large diamond solitaire on a golden chain.

"I wish that Monsieur Redding will place 'imself in a comfortable chair," she commanded. "And I will sit 'ere across from him."

She then commenced to speak to Nigel, explaining step-by-step what she was about to do. Elisande watched her brother apprehensively. If he did not relax and cooperate, nothing would come of this attempt.

"Don't look so worried." Lord Raven had come to stand beside her. "I've seen Madame in action, remember. I promise there'll be no ill effects."

"I wish you could convince Nigel of that," Elisande sighed. Then she added, "Mme Benoit is not what I expected."

"Did you think she'd be a snaggle-toothed crone mumbling incantations?" His lordship slid a hand under Elisande's elbow and led her to the shadows near the door. "Mme Benoit is connected to the Comtesse Fegere and is the widow of a wealthy banker," he went on. "She numbers royalty amongst her clients."

Meaning that the Reddings were hardly what Madame was used to. "*How* did you persuade her to come all this way for Nigel?" she wondered.

"It wasn't only for Nigel that she came." Lord Raven stopped himself barely in time. He had almost told Elisande that it was for her peace of mind that he had paid Madame's enormous fee.

She should have guessed that the handsome Frenchwoman in her jet and diamonds had come to Dorset because of Lord Raven. Obviously she was the sort of female his lordship admired. It was not surprising, and yet Elisande was conscious of a bitter taste in her mouth.

Deliberately turning away from the mesmerist, she noted that the marquess had stationed himself next to Constance and was watching Nigel closely. The marquess's usually good-natured face was hard with suspicion.

Lord Raven followed the direction of her gaze. "I'm sorry about Wigram," he apologized. "I tried my best to stop him from coming, but he's got a maggot in his brain that Nigel will break down and confess, and he wants to be in at the kill." Elisande winced. "If I hadn't brought him, Wigram would have no doubt appeared in the middle of the treatment and ruined everything."

The mesmerist was explaining to Nigel that she would put him in a trance that would take him into the past. "Can she really do as she says?" Elisande asked.

Her voice cracked with nerves, and Raven felt an almost irresistible urge to put his arm around her shoulders. This protective instinct was heightened when he saw the sleepless shadows beneath her eyes.

Abruptly he said, "You are making yourself ill

over something over which you have no control. No matter what happens today, you must go on with your life." He watched her eyes fix on Nigel's face and added, "*Your* life, I mean. There's a time when you have to think of yourself."

"Would *you* abandon your brother?" she demanded.

"I'm going to." He sounded almost grim, and she saw that his eyes were hard with determination. "I've received a letter from my manager in Salem. There are some matters I want to oversee myself, so I've told Wigram that whatever happens tonight, I'm for the New World."

"How I envy you!"

Raven looked at her sharply, but before he could speak Mme Benoit commanded silence. "*Allons, nous commençons,*" she announced. "We begin. Now there will be no distractions, *vous comprenez?*"

She lifted the diamond around her neck and, holding it by its chain, began to swing it slightly. "Monsieur Redding, kindly follow the diamond with your eyes," she directed. "Do not take your gaze away from it."

The fire burned lower and shadows crept into the little cottage as Mme Benoit crooned, "All you see is the lights from the diamond. You will ignore all else. Can you do that?" Nigel assented. "Now, count for me back from twenty to one, Monsieur Redding. As I told you, when you reach the number one, you will be fast asleep."

Nigel twisted in his chair. *Not bloody likely*, his body language said. His voice was vigorous as he began to count in obedience to the mesmerist's instructions.

"Your arms are heavy. Your legs are heavy. Your head is so heavy you can hardly hold it up," Mme Benoit murmured. "Do not fight it—let your head droop, and let your eyelids close."

"Twelve, eleven, ten, nine," Nigel droned. His voice was lower now. Lower still as it went on. Lord Raven touched Elisande's arm as Nigel's head began to sink onto his chest.

"Your eyes are closed now, but you see the light of the diamond dancing in your mind. It will serve to light the road down the past."

"Five, four, three, two—"

Elisande held her breath, but the *one* did not come. "Are you sleeping, monsieur?" Mme Benoit asked in her rich, low voice. No answer. "Answer me, if you please, but without awakening," she went on. "*Enfin*, are you sleeping?"

"Asleep," Nigel muttered.

"*Bon.* Now, we will make a journey together, yes? Back nineteen months ago to the night of the thirtieth of March, 1815." A pause. "Where are you on this night?"

"At Hanard House. I've come with dispatches from the Duke of Wellington."

Nigel spoke drowsily, and Elisande's heart gave a painful lurch. She could dimly see the others in the darkened room: the marquess, openly skeptical, rocking on his heels; Constance, standing with her hands clasped as if in prayer, Parse half-in and half-out of the kitchen, with a look of deep apprehension on his knobby face.

In a low but perfectly distinct voice, Nigel was saying, "The dispatches are for Colonel Hanard."

"They are important, these dispatches?"

"Crucial. Boney's on the prowl again, and Wellington's sent us our orders. But a party's going on here at Hanard House—lots of people everywhere. My Sylvia likes parties."

"Deuced cheek," the marquess was heard to mutter.

"Sylvia looks beautiful tonight. Wearing a black Spanish dress and Spanish combs in her hair."

"Are any other ladies there at the party?" Mme Benoit asked.

"None so beautiful as Sylvia. She's dancing with Sir Rupert Vole. Vole owns lots of land and has warm pockets. If only I were rich enough to pay my addresses to her."

Skillfully Mme Benoit guided Nigel away from Miss Hanard and back to the party. She made him describe many of the guests and through his eyes they saw Lady Anabelle Graymount, then a dashing young widow surrounded by a circle of admirers.

"Where is the colonel?" the mesmerist then asked.

"He's come to greet me. Knows that a big engagement's coming with Boney on the loose." Nigel paused to emphasize, "Frogs would kill to know what's in these dispatches. Hanard's going to lock them up in the safe."

Remember, Elisande begged her brother silently, but at the same time she felt an almost palpable fear. Nigel's quiet, sleepwalking voice vividly recalled his nightmares.

She listened fearfully as Nigel described the scene during which the dispatches had been locked up in the safe. Then he said, "Going back to the dancing, now. We meet Lady Graymount in the hall. Colonel asks Lady Graymount for the cotillion, and we go to the great room together. Think the colonel has a *tendre* for Lady Anabelle."

The tone of mild amusement in Nigel's voice shifted to frustration as he described time passing while he attempted to dance with Sylvia. "No use— every dance's taken," he said adding, "can't *stand* watching her dance with other men. Going out to smoke in the garden." He pantomimed pulling out a cigar. "Wait a minute—no matches. Must have dropped them in the colonel's study."

Everyone, including the marquess watched anxiously as Nigel's feet pantomimed walking. "What are you doing now?" Mme Benoit wondered.

"I'm standing in the garden, thinking. I love Miss Hanard with all my heart—but I'll never win her hand unless I can become a rich man. Or a famous one. Maybe now that Boney's on the march again, I can distinguish myself in battle. It's happened before."

"This is old ground, so far," Lord Raven whispered to Elisande, as Nigel fell silent. Even at such a moment, she was acutely aware that he was standing so close to her that she could feel his warm breath on her cheek. "We've both heard all this before."

After he spent quite some time in the garden, Nigel had decided to return to the colonel's study and find his matches. "Walking into the study now. Now where are those damned matches—eh, *what's this?*"

Elisande fairly jumped at the different note in her brother's voice. "The book—*Memoirs of Hadrian*—it's lying open on the desk. The spare key's gone. My God, the safe—"

He leaned forward in slack-jawed horror. "The dispatches—they're gone! The safe's empty! Oh, my God. Hell and all the devils. Someone has taken the dispatches."

"What do you do now?" Mme Benoit asked.

"Must do *something*. But wait—perhaps the colonel has them. Must go downstairs and find him."

Involuntarily Elisande took a step backward, closing the small distance between her and Lord Raven. He put a supporting arm around her, but she was not even conscious of his touch as Mme Benoit asked, "Do you find the colonel?"

"No—can't find him. My God. Oh, my God. I run down the hall back to the dancing. Can't see him—

can't see Sylvia, either. Perhaps he's in the garden. Dark out here now; hard to see."

"Is the colonel there, *mon ami?*" Mme Benoit asked as the young man's jerky sentences trailed into silence.

"No. No one here. Stop a minute, someone's walking down the Cliff Path ahead of me. A woman—" His voice rose in recognition and profound relief. "It's Sylvia. Sylvia will know where her father is."

"How do you know it is Miss Hanard, monsieur? Can you see her face?"

"Too dark to see her face, but don't have to. Combs in her hair catch the lamplight from the house. I'll follow her down the Cliff Path, catch up to her."

"Explain to us what is the 'Cliff Path'?" the mesmerist directed.

"It's a path that starts in the Hanards' garden and leads through the woods to the cliffs. It's about a ten-minute walk, but not an easy one at night." Nigel's voice tightened. "Sylvia, it's dangerous to walk here without a lantern. You'll hurt yourself— damn it, she doesn't hear me."

Nigel's feet were making running movements now. "Tell us where you are, *mon ami.*" Mme Benoit directed.

"I've followed Sylvia to the cliffs. She's going *down* the steps now, to the beach below. Worried she'll be frightened and fall if I call out, so I follow her down until—wait a minute, though—there's a boat of some kind anchored there and—good God!"

Elisande's skin crawled at the change in Nigel's voice. "There's a man down there waiting," he gritted. "Sylvia's running to meet him. They're talking in *French*! Sylvia, what are you doing? No—can't be—she's giving him a package of papers. On my life, she's handing over Wellington's dispatches."

"It's a lie—has to be!"

The marquess's cry of protest ended abruptly as the mesmerist ordered him to hold his tongue. "What now, Monsieur Redding?" she asked. "What happens now?"

"Now he's giving her *money*," Nigel groaned.

So it had been Sylvia Hanard all the time. Elisande felt as if the floor was tilting beneath her. She clung tightly to Lord Raven's supporting arm as his lordship said quietly, "You wanted to know the truth. Listen, Elisande."

Nigel was raging, "Must be a mistake. He's forced her to do this. That's it—his fault. I'll kill the brute! *Stop, you!* But there are others. Many others. Men with sticks and cudgels. They're beating me. Must fight them off—can't let them get away with those dispatches—ah!"

Nigel fell back into his chair. "Fainted, by gad," the marquess's shaken voice observed. "Don't blame him—close on faintin' myself."

Elisande started to go to her brother, but Raven held her back. "He is still in the past," he reminded her sternly. "Let Madame bring him back."

Shaken and faint herself, Elisande listened as the mesmerist guided Nigel back to the present. "You are returning to us now, to October twenty-fourth, 1816. You will return with all memory of what has happened clear in your mind. The wall of forgetfulness is no more. Count with me back from ten, and when you reach one, you will awaken refreshed, as from a deep and restful sleep."

Once more Nigel began to count. Elisande heard his voice through a tangle of emotions. What Nigel had at last remembered made a great deal of sense, for it would not have been difficult for Sylvia Hanard to learn where her father had kept the spare key to the safe. The wicked girl had sold those dispatches to the French and then, when

Nigel discovered her perfidy, had stood by while he was beaten almost to death.

"How could she do it?"

Nigel's tortured outcry echoed Elisande's own thought. She broke loose from Lord Raven and ran to her brother, but springing to his feet he pushed past her and strode toward the door. Parse ran after him and caught him by the arm. "Steady, Captain, sir," he muttered.

"Parse—it was Sylvia all along." Hardly conscious of what he did, Nigel shook the big Yorkshireman. "She let them beat me and leave me for dead. Let them put that dispatch in my pocket so that the colonel'd think that I was the traitor. On my life, she did it—and I'd have died for her."

"And all this time, she has let you live in pain and dishonor," Constance growled. Her mild eyes sparkled with anger. "That—that wicked minx. But at least now you remember, Nigel. At least your name can be cleared now."

But Nigel's face, when he turned to face them, was more hagridden than ever before. Brushing past Parse, he opened the door and walked out, closing it after him.

Elisande followed at once. Constance would have gone also, but Lord Raven stopped her. "Let him go for now, Miss Dayton. Nigel's got back his memory, and now he has to deal with it—alone."

He looked hard at his brother as he spoke, and the marquess gave a shaky little nod. "Deal with it—I say, yes, must deal with it," he mumbled. "Never would have believed that Miss Hanard could—I've been blind. Blind as a—as a deuced bat."

"I should follow Elisande," Constance said, and Parse added fiercely that his captain needed him.

"Stay here, and I'll go after them both," Lord Raven directed.

He walked out of the cottage and saw Nigel striding down the village road. Elisande was hurrying after him.

Raven quickened his step and caught up with her saying, "Leave your brother alone. He wanted to remember, and now he has."

"But no one expected that he would remember such terrible things," Elisande mourned. "Sylvia Hanard, of all people. I would never have guessed it."

"Nor I," Lord Raven agreed. "I'd never have believed that the spoiled chit had it in her to plan and carry out such an undertaking. To keep silent about it all this time requires a cool blood that I had never expected from the temperamental Miss Hanard."

"But she did keep silent. She did. Now what will become of Nigel?"

"I'd say that was up to him." Elisande looked up quickly at his tone, and Lord Raven added, "He has to decide what to do with his life, Elisande. So must you."

The sound of her name on his lips curved about her heart like a tender hand. Elisande felt that treacherous heart beat more swiftly as his lordship continued, "Nigel now knows he's no traitor, so my guess is that he'll have no more nightmares. Wigram will finally get over his so-called love. We can safely leave out brothers to their own devices."

She did not look in the least convinced, so he added, "There must be things you want to do with your life. You said you envied me a few minutes ago. Why not visit the New World yourself?"

It took a moment for what he was saying to register, and that was followed by a moment of wonder. In that heartbeat's fragment of time, Elisande let her mind wander free and saw the wide ocean, and the storms, and the stars at sea. She saw the sun rise over a fair new coastline, felt the shadow of trees that had stood tall since the beginning of time.

Raven was dazzled by the soft wonder that filled her eyes. He had spoken those words as an illustration, not an invitation. Yet, now he realized that he had spoken from his heart.

Why not? he asked himself. With Elisande at his side, the voyage to Salem would prove ten times more exciting. The stars would be brighter. Together with this lovely, spirited woman he—no, *they* could achieve, taste, see, *live*.

Lord Raven's heart swelled on that thought. "Elisande, come with me," he said. "I love you."

There was no answer. Thinking that he had shocked her, he searched her face and saw that she was staring past him down the road.

"Nigel is coming back," she exclaimed.

She had not even heard him. Her entire attention was on the young man who was now walking rapidly back toward them. Lord Raven bit his lip as Elisande picked up her skirts and hurried forward to meet her brother crying, "Nigel, I know that this has been such a bitter blow for you—"

He interrupted her. "It was wrong of me to rush off like that. Won't solve anything."

Nigel paused and drew painful breath. "But I had to think it through, d'you see? Realize now that seeing—seeing *her* sell those dispatches was too hard to bear. Made myself forget it ever happened. On my life, Lisa, there really was a 'wall' in my mind, as that Frenchwoman said."

Bitterness filled Elisande's voice. "And all this time Sylvia Hanard has allowed you to believe yourself disgraced. I hate her. But now at last the end is in sight."

Clearing Nigel's name would not be easy, Elisande knew, but it could be done. "General Lear headed the board of inquiry," she began. "You yourself said that he was sympathetic to you. I know he will listen to us—and to the testimony of Lord Raven and the marquess. And he will question that despicable woman—"

"No," Nigel said.

"No?"

"We've got to go back to Sussex," Nigel said. A muscle twitched in his lean cheek, but apart from that he appeared perfectly calm. "I'm not going to write to General Lear. I'm not going to say a word about what—what I remembered to anyone. And neither are you."

For a moment she stared at him. Then she cried, "But, Nigel, you must! What did we come to Sussex for, if not to clear your name?"

"Because I thought that regaining my memory would free me. Lisa, remembering's ten times worse than any nightmare I ever had. The thought that Sylvia—" he broke off, shaking his head almost wildly. "On my life, I can't do it."

Elisande felt ready to scream. "But, Nigel," she cried, "think! Collect how much suffering that woman has caused."

"Lisa, I still love her."

"Nigel!"

"Couldn't bear her being in disgrace," Nigel said. In a low tone he continued, "She couldn't stand being despised by society. She'll—she won't be able to survive, Lisa. Promise me you'll keep my secret."

He turned to Lord Raven, standing and watching silently. "You understand why this must be so, don't you?"

Lord Raven was looking at Elisande's white face. "It is your decision to make," he said quietly.

"Then you *agree* with him?" Lord Raven said nothing, and all the emotions that had been gathering force within Elisande exploded into words. "I am glad that his lordship understands you, Nigel, because I do not. Con and I have risked much and spent much and given up a great deal in order to clear your name. Parse was ready to give his life for you. How can you remain silent now?"

Nigel had gone white to the lips. "I know what all of you have done for me. Never will forget it—on my life, I intend to make it up to you." He squared his shoulders and then added sternly, "I'll find work in London—or in Wales, perhaps. It'd be better for you and Con if I don't live with you and bring shame to you."

"You know we will never let you go to London or anywhere else," Elisande cried, beside herself. "We are a family, and we stand or fall together. But, Nigel, are you willing to expose yourself to more pain and disgrace simply to shield a heartless girl who does not care a straw for you?"

"Yes," Nigel said. He added passionately, "Lisa, you don't understand—can't—because you're not in love yourself. You don't choose those you give your heart to, sister, it happens. Can't explain it anymore than that—but I'm not going to say a word against Sylvia Hanard—and you aren't either."

He strode past her toward the cottage. Elisande stood where she was. The fight had drained out of her and she felt as limp as a rag. It had all been for nothing—no, worse than nothing.

"Leave him alone," Lord Raven's quiet voice said. "He's made his decision, now respect it." He paused to add, "Wigram won't say anything either—he certainly won't want any scandal. He'll withdraw his suit, and we'll be on our way back to Scotland."

"Just as you planned," she murmured.

He frowned. "I didn't plan *this*. Play fair, Elisande."

She drew a deep breath and fought for calm. "I did not mean to sound ungrateful. You have been more than kind, and—and it is not your fault that what happened did happen."

She paused and attempted a smile. "I wish you Godspeed and joy of the sea and the New World."

The words Raven had spoken before rose to his lips, but something made him hold back. "You mean to go back to Sussex, then?" he probed.

She nodded. "Con and I will try and persuade Nigel to remain with us. He needs us more than ever and—and we will come out of this if we all hold together."

It was only a matter of putting his arms around her, and she would be close against him as she had been last night. The need to hold her, taste her lips, feel her warm softness against him, was almost unbearable. But this time Raven forced himself to think logically and clearly.

As she had freely admitted, Elisande was bound to her family. As long as this fierce loyalty kept her prisoner, their worlds were as far apart as the north and south poles. Raven thought of small English villages and the boring sameness of such an existence. He might as well spend his time at Tanner and listen to Wigram nattering on about fruit trees and apiaries.

Raven realized that he had been on the point of committing an idiocy. He had actually been ready to declare himself. And by so doing, Raven knew, he would have leg shackled himself not only to Elisande but also to her hagridden brother. The thought was horrifying.

"I hope that you will have a safe journey, Miss Redding," Lord Raven said in a suddenly formal voice, and she thanked him with a simple dignity that gave him pause. In her way, Raven thought, Elisande Redding was a greater lady than Mme Benoit herself.

He could not help asking, "Will you be all right?"

She could not read the expression in his eyes. Did he really care? Elisande wondered numbly. But, of course, he was merely being courteous. Now that his objective had been reached, Lord Raven was impatient to be gone.

"We will manage," she said and then added, "thank you again for all your help."

But even while she was saying those prosaic words, Elisande thought of strong arms holding her close and of passionate lips and the feel of sea wind in her hair. She understood Nigel far better than he thought, for even now Lord Raven's kisses kindled a dark fire in her blood.

Falling in love with an adventuresome lord had not been her intention, but in spite of her it had happened—happened simply and quite irrevocably. And though she was certain that she would never see Lord Raven again, Elisande knew that she would love him all her days.

Chapter Ten

"*Tchah*—take the foul thing away. I said I wasn't going to wear it, and I deuced won't."

"Truly, may lord, we are most testy today."

Sniffing disapproval through his thin nose, Landers picked up the woolen scarf that the marquess had flung to the ground. "May I bring to your lordship's attention that it is extraordinarily cold today?" he asked coldly. "Since your lordship will be riding in Lord Raven's curricle, your lordship must cover the throat at all times."

"Bah!"

"Your lordship cannot wish to fall victim to the grippe. Or to an inflammation of the lungs. The scarf, may lord—it must be the scarf."

The marquess leaned back, folded obstinate arms across his plump chest, and announced that he did not give a tinker's curse about any paltry illness. "Take that deuced thing away—and yourself with it, too. I don't want to lay eyes on either of you 'til we get to Scotland."

Fairly quivering with insult, Landers stalked off.

"Deuced tyrant," the marquess muttered. "Give him a bit of his deuced own back, the muffin-faced wag-feather."

He looked up at Lord Raven, who had walked in during this exchange. "It's done?"

"Done. The *Silver Raven* has set sail and is ferrying Mme Benoit back to France, and I've just told

Hanard that you wish to withdraw your suit. Are you ready to push on, Wigram?"

The marquess regarded his younger brother with an admiration tinged with envy. How was it, he wondered, that no matter what crisis presented itself, Ivo met it looking done up to a cow's thumb, trim as a trencher, and in the indisputable kick of fashion? He himself had spent the morning biting his nails by the fire, whilst there stood his brother in his dove gray square-tailed coat, buff breeches, gleaming Hessians, and handsome dark riding cloak looking as if he had been taking a refreshing stroll around the park.

"Did Hanard kick up a lot of dust?" he asked. "I say, Ivo, it was deuced good of you—goin' to see the man on my behalf, mean to say. Plain truth of it is, didn't think I could stand goin' to Hanard House and takin' the chance of seein' *her* again."

He walked unsteadily to the sideboard, poured a healthy measure of brandy, and offered the glass to his brother who said impatiently, "It won't do to let the horses stand for too long, Wigram. *Are* you ready to leave?" When the marquess nodded, he added, "No, Hanard didn't say much at all. I explained that you were a patient man but that since Miss Hanard obviously didn't want to marry you, you did not wish to cause her undue distress. Et cetera, et cetera. The colonel seemed resigned."

As the marquess drained his brandy, Lord Raven added as an afterthought, "He looked hagged though, and no wonder. Now he needs to find another son-in-law with warm pockets."

Nor was the colonel the only one who looked hagridden, Lord Raven thought. Since Nigel's disclosure yesterday afternoon, Wigram had hardly been himself.

Shock had turned him pasty faced when he had learned that his beloved Sylvia had been in Napoleon's pay, and on return to the Gilded Stag had been so *distrait* that Landers had produced pills made of spider's web and a medicinal drink made of wormwood and herbs infused in beer. To these hideous ministrations the marquess had submitted so meekly that even Raven had become worried.

Since then Wigram had remained mump faced and gloomy and had left all the details of breaking off his distasteful engagement in his younger brother's hands. This Lord Raven had gladly done—and now at last they were about to leave Dorset.

"The sooner we leave the better," he urged. His brother sighed deeply. "Wigram, you can't be such a fool as to still nurse a *tendre* for that jade?"

The marquess looked horrified. "A *tendre* for Miss Hanard? Oh, good God, no. I say, Ivo, I feel like such a fool. To have thought that a girl just out of the nursery would want to be leg shackled to a deuced old duffer like me—wonder why you didn't tell me I was makin' a cake of myself."

"I did. Several times."

The marquess scowled and stared into the near distance. "You're right, Ivo. High time to go home," he said without conviction. "Only—" he sighed yet again and chewed his upper lip.

"It's over and done with, Wigram. Put it behind you, man. There're plenty of fish in the sea."

"Fine of you to talk," quoth the marquess grumpily. "You're going *back* to the sea. I say, Ivo, ain't you too old to be junketin' about the world? Time to settle down with a nice female. Like that Miss Redding, for instance. She's a right 'un if I ever saw one."

"Is that what you think?"

The ice in his lordship's voice penetrated even his brother's thick hide. He glanced uneasily at Lord Raven and muttered that Ivo and the lady had spent a great deal of time together, after all. "Seemed as if you was drawn together. Could've been mistook, of course," he added in some haste.

"You're mistaken. Miss Redding and I spent time together in *your* service." Lord Raven directed a quelling look at the marquess and repeated, "It was in *your* service, Wigram, that we were 'drawn together,' as you put it. Now our brief association is over."

"Over—that's it, over," the marquess echoed gloomily. "Miss Redding's goin' home along with Miss Dayton."

He did not sigh this time, but something in his voice caused Lord Raven, who had been on his way out of the door, to stop and look back at his brother. Surprise gave way to understanding. "I see," he murmured.

"Of course you do. I could never keep anythin' from you, Ivo. Always a downy one, you were." The marquess rubbed his stubby nose as he added eagerly, "I say, ain't Miss Dayton a fine female? Interestin' to talk to—mean to say, she talks about things that interest a fellow. Good to talk to, good to look at, too, in a fine, friendly way. Like a cheerful fire in the hearth greetin' a fellow at the end of the day. Deuced clever, too, with all those books she's always readin', but she don't use her cleverness to make a fellow feel stupid. Always bindin' him up when he's hurt and dishin' up deuced fine little teas with the jolliest kinds of honey, too. Would think bees'd turn themselves inside out tryin' to please her, that's what I say."

Lord Raven did not try to make sense of this confused monologue. "Have you told Miss Dayton your feelings?" he asked when the marquess had rambled into silence.

"You may be a downy one, Ivo, but you're far afield here. Far afield." The marquess sighed so deeply that the tips of his collar quivered. "Don't forget how I was throwin' sheep's eyes at Miss Hanard a few days ago. When I think of how I went on natterin' to Miss Dayton about Sylvia Hanard—"

He broke off, poured himself another brandy, and tossed it down in a single gulp. "D'you think any self-respectin' female would listen to me?" he then resumed in a slightly slurred voice. "How can I call off a match with one female and then go and ask to pay m'addresses to another?"

For once Lord Raven had no answers ready. While Wigram was talking, he had been remembering the almost incredible desire he had felt to gather Elisande Redding into his arms. It had been an almost primitive longing, like a man's love for the sea.

"You've been handed a nasty jolt by that red-haired minx," he said aloud. "You're on the rebound, which is a dangerous time in a man's life. A time when a man's most vulnerable, Wigram. It's happened to me once or twice before."

The marquess was hanging on his brother's words. "And you lived through it?" he asked hopefully. "I say, Ivo, that's deuced reassurin'. Mean to say—maybe I'll come out of this, too."

"Of course you will." Lord Raven smiled at his brother and attempted to recall the beauties with whom he had conducted amorous liaisons in years passed. Not one of them came to mind. Instead, he saw an eager face tilted skyward to watch swans in flight and tasted soft lips sweeter than honey mixed with wine.

"Of course you will," he repeated heartily. "Memories fade, Wigram. Mark my words, old fellow—in a year or two you won't even remember what Miss Dayton looked like."

* * *

It had all been for nothing, after all.

That thought hurt most amongst all the other great and little hurts that filtered through Elisande's mind as she stood packing her trunk in the tiny bedroom she shared with Constance. Outside, she could hear Parse whistling cheerfully. He, at least, was delighted that they were returning "back home." But for the rest of them—

No, nothing had changed. The world still regarded Nigel a traitor, while Nigel himself remained sick at heart. And the Reddings were still poor—but wait, here at last was a change, for they were poorer than when they came to Dorset.

She wondered how they could manage back in Sussex. Their old house would be waiting for them, with the dubious welcome of accumulated dust, bare cupboards, and the threat of winter to come. Parse had negotiated with a neighbor in the village for the lease of a trap that would take them to Allford. From Allford they would take the stage, and the cost of travel plus the last payment of rent to Mrs. Willoughby would leave precious little capital.

"I will find work," Elisande said stoutly. "Lady Carme cannot be the only one who is in need of a governess. We will sort it out somehow."

"Are you talking to yourself?" Constance asked. She came into the room and sat down on her bed between two bags of neatly packed books. "When I am making my teas, I often carry on conversations with myself. But then eccentric behavior is expected from an ape leader like me."

Her smile faded, and she drew a deep breath that was almost a sigh. "I wish we were not going away this afternoon."

"I did not know you were so fond of Dorset," Elisande said. As she folded her worn nightgown into her trunk, she added, "You have always said that Willoughby Cottage is too small for us."

"The cottage is small and cramped and inconvenient, but a home is not just a structure made of stone and wood." Constance clasped her hands in her lap as she added earnestly, "It is the people who live inside the house that make it special."

"You are a wise woman, Con."

"Oh, no," Constance said, flushing at the compliment and going very gruff. "I am stupid. Don't regard me, dear Elisande. But I wish we were not leaving just yet. You see, the cards have finally decided to become communicative. They've told me that we have unfinished business here."

Lately Constance had been bemoaning the fact that her tarot cards had given nothing but ambivalent and contradictory statements. "What else did they say?" Elisande asked absently.

"They are still very vague, but perhaps it is because I am so confused myself," Constance declared. "This morning I first drew the Priestess crossed by the Nine of Rods—which means that there will be happiness tinged with the unexpected. Then I drew the Fool, and that seems to say that we are taking a short journey over water." She paused to add, "Our route to Sussex lies over land, so that prediction is manifestly untrue. But no matter how often I tried, the same cards kept coming up."

She looked so disturbed that Elisande spoke bracingly. "Your cards hit the mark on one thing, Con. We do have unfinished business here. I have been thinking that after all that Anabelle Hanard did to help us, I at least owe her the courtesy of a call."

Constance's small brown eyes opened wide. "You mean, go to Hanard House? Is it not wiser to send a note instead?"

"A note may fall into the wrong hands and cause trouble for Anabelle," Elisande pointed out. "I feel we owe her an explanation. We have an hour before we must leave, so I will go now."

Constance watched doubtfully as Elisande closed the lid of her small trunk and reached for the old bonnet which dangled by the door of the bedroom. "Do you mean to tell Mrs. Hanard about Mme Benoit?"

Elisande shook her head. "We have promised Nigel to say nothing about Sylvia's treachery. But I can—and will—tell Anabelle that Nigel now knows he is innocent. That much I can say at least."

Constance considered this as Elisande settled the bonnet on her head. "I will come with you," she offered.

"I will be glad for the company, but I thought you disliked the idea of going to Hanard House."

Flushed but determined, Constance nodded. "I feel that I must come with you," she said. "Along with the Three of Rods, I drew the Hierophant next to the Justice card. *That* message is plain: I must do what I must do."

The hired trap stood in front of the little cottage. Elisande stroked the nose of the stout horse that was nibbling at Mrs. Willoughby's flowers, and looked around for Parse, but the big Yorkshireman was nowhere to be found.

"Nigel is not here either, so perhaps they have gone off together," she said. "Never mind, Con. We'll be back long before it is time to leave."

Constance climbed into the trap beside her cousin and, with a heartfelt request to drive safely, settled down into a brown study which lasted until, almost at the outskirts of the village, a familiar voice hailed them.

Some distance away the Widow Willoughby was

walking with her daughter. The widow was in her usual black weeds, but Harriet—

"Good heavens, Con," Elisande exclaimed, "that child is wearing a dress!"

She stared at Harriet, whose hair was brushed and combed, and who wore a dress and even an apron. As she and Alexander approached the Reddings' trap, Elisande noted that the dress looked oddly familiar.

"Is that not one of *your* morning dresses, Con?" she wondered.

Constance said gruffly, "It was too worn to wear but good enough to cut down for the child. I promised her a treat if she learned her letters. Which she did, and very quickly, too."

She smiled shyly at Harriet, who was asking anxiously, "Is it true you're going away today, Miss Con?"

"I am afraid so," Constance said, "but you must promise to continue reading in the book I gave you. You are very clever, you know."

"And pretty, too," Elisande added with a smile.

Harriet grinned self-consciously, attempted to put her hands into her pockets, found none, and put them behind her back instead. "I wish you wasn't going," she said almost as gruffly as Constance. "Everybody's going away, seems like." She hooked a thumb toward her mother. "Ma's all hupset 'cause Mr. Parse's leaving, too. Been looking for 'im since this morning, she 'as."

The widow's exclamations of protest drowned out conversation for several minutes. "I dunno what's got into this child," she went on in an aggrieved tone. "If I've been looking for Mr. Parse, it's to tell 'im that there's been word that the Marquess Tanner's leaving town along o' 'is brother. The wedding's orf."

She had naturally expected Lord Raven to shake

the dust of Dorset as soon as he possibly could—and who could blame the marquess for being in a hurry to leave the scene of his humiliation? And yet the news carried a sting. It was astonishing, Elisande thought, how much that sting could hurt.

"It's time we were on our way," she said aloud. "Parse and Nigel will expect us back within the hour, and we must say our good-byes to Anabelle."

She and Constance bowed to the curtsying Mrs. Willoughby and drove away. "You are a miracle worker, Con," Elisande said as they bowled down the road. "Not only did you teach Harriet how to read, but she is a different child. You are a natural teacher."

"Harriet only needed someone to believe in her," Constance said earnestly. "Elisande, I have been thinking that when we return to Sussex, perhaps we could open a school, you and I. It would serve to bring in some money, and I would enjoy the work enormously."

In spite of her brave words, Constance's voice was touched with sadness. When Elisande turned to glance at her, she saw that large tears were trickling down her cousin's cheeks. "What is it, Con? What's wrong?" Elisande asked in alarm.

Constance whisked out her handkerchief and dabbed at her eyes. "I have got something in my eye," she muttered. And then she added, "No, that is not it at all. Oh, Elisande, he has gone away without even saying good-bye."

She buried her face in her handkerchief and sobbed aloud. Elisande stopped the horses at the side of the road and gathered her cousin into her arms.

"I never thought it was for me," Constance wept. "I thought that falling in love was something that happened to other people—people who are prettier and younger. But then *he* came."

"The Marquess Tanner," Elisande murmured.

Constance nodded against her cousin's shoulder. "It was all rainbow chasing, of course. He had—I am persuaded that he has no idea about my feelings. It was, as the books say, an unrequited *tendre*. *He* was always in love with that—that horrid, redheaded minx."

Feeling sick at heart, Elisande stroked Constance's back. She wished that there was something she could say, but she knew no words could heal an aching heart.

"I only tell you because we are all going away and I will never see him again." Constance drew away from Elisande and put a small, plump hand on her bosom. "It hurts me *here* to think that I will never see him again," she added simply.

Elisande's own eyes had filled with tears. "I know."

"I thought you might," Constance gruffed. "I could not be sure, but I *believed* that you had come to have feelings for Lord Raven. His lordship is so clever and strong and handsome and assured that any woman would be justified in being dazzled by him. Even my clever, strong, resourceful, and beautiful cousin."

Laughing through her own tears, Elisande picked up the reins. "You are trying to turn me up sweet. I may have been dazzled, as you say, but I always knew *au fond* that it would lead to nothing. Lord Raven is not for me and never will be."

"It is the same for me and Wigram—I always called him that to myself," Constance confessed. Her cheeks became very flushed as she added earnestly, "He is not handsome or strong or even very clever, but then neither am I. We enjoy the same things. He loves animals and bees and fruit trees, so we always had something to talk about. I lent him my books, and he said he enjoyed them. No doubt," she added with a sigh, "he considered me a stuffy old antidote and a bluestocking to boot."

"Nonsense. I am persuaded that he liked you tremendously. Why else would he have hung about the cottage?"

Constance brightened for a moment, then shook her head. "I suspect he came because he was trying to find some way to discredit Nigel and thus further his cause with that scheming jade. When I think of her, I become so angry that I would like to box her ears."

"So would I. Only, Con—" Elisande hesitated, trying to frame a thought that had been troubling her for some time, "Does it not seem even a little strange to you? Sylvia Hanard doesn't seem to be the sort of person who would be a spy for the French."

"But she was," Constance pointed out. "Long ago the tarot told us that things were not what they seem. They must have been referring to that brazen hussy. She fooled us all."

Elisande was not satisfied. "I have been thinking. Why should Sylvia do anything so dangerous for money? I am sure she never wanted for anything."

"For the fun of it, perhaps. Some women are born adventuresses, and Miss Hanard is very bold."

"I can imagine her falling in love with some dashing officer in Napoleon's army and throwing everything to the winds so that she could run away with him. That sort of drama would appeal to her. But selling her country for money is a cold and calculated act." Elisande paused to add thoughtfully, "Lord Raven said so, too. He wondered that Sylvia had been capable of something so cold and deliberate."

Constance frowned. "You must collect that Lord Raven also said that the colonel doesn't have a lot of money these days. Sylvia Hanard likes fine clothes and jewels."

As Constance spoke, they arrived at Hanard House where a wooden-faced footman announced that madam was not at home. Elisande was on the point of leaving a card and a message when a familiar voice called from the garden.

Sylvia Hanard was waving at them. She was dressed in a sea green walking-out suit of the newest fashion, and over it wore a pelisse of the same color trimmed with swansdown. A pretty hat of chip straw decorated with cream-colored cabbage roses sat jauntily atop her red hair. A strand of large, perfectly matching pearls hung about her neck.

Anger, so strong as to be physically sickening, flared in Elisande. Sylvia looked as though she had not a care in the world. She was oblivious to the suffering of the man who had condemned himself to years of torment for her sake. And she was obviously going out, for behind her walked a maid carrying a cloak and gloves.

"Elisande—I am glad you are here," she exclaimed. "I want to talk to you."

Constance glared in silence. Elisande replied curtly, "We came to call on Mrs. Hanard."

"Stepmama's not here." Sylvia added imperiously, "Come into the garden with me—I do need to talk to you."

"I doubt that we have anything to say to each other," Elisande turned determinedly toward the trap. "Come, Con."

"*Please!*" Sylvia's hauteur vanished, and her voice trembled. When Elisande turned her head, she saw that tears were brimming up in Miss Hanard's eyes. "*Please* come into the garden for a moment."

The Redding women exchanged glances, and

Constance shrugged slightly. "Perhaps we should hear what she has to say," she gruffed.

Silently they followed Sylvia into the garden. "You caught me just as I was preparing to leave," the colonel's daughter began.

Elisande looked hard at Sylvia and tried to picture her as a heartless jade and a scheming traitress, but something in her mind remained unwilling to accept this.

"We should not detain you," Constance was growling.

"You don't understand," Sylvia cried. "I was riding down to the village to see *you*. Is it true that you are leaving?" Elisande nodded. "And Nigel—is he going, too? And without a thought of me?"

"On the contrary, he thinks too much about you—" Constance stopped, gave Elisande a defensive look, and lapsed into moody silence.

"Then—it is over. He has given up." Sylvia sat down abruptly on a marble bench and covered her face with her hands. Her slender shoulders shuddered with sobs.

"Crying never mended fences," gruffed Constance, but Elisande asked, "Who told you that we were going away?"

"Everyone knows," Sylvia replied in a muffled voice. "Lord Raven was here this morning—Papa was in *such* a temper—to say that his brother was crying off. Afterward, my abigail went into the village and found that the Marquess Farmer and Lord Raven were leaving. That *you* were leaving, too."

Sylvia paused to draw a deep breath. "Papa was so hateful about it. He said that at least this time we were finished with the traitor—meaning Nigel."

"No doubt you believe that he is a traitor, too," Elisande could not help retorting.

Sylvia threw up her head and regarded the other

woman with a scowling, tear-blotched face. "How dare you say that? You know I believe him innocent. Oh, *why* is Nigel going away without a word to me?"

Elisande put her hands on the redhead's shoulders and looked hard into her swimming emerald eyes. "Because he remembered about that night. Do you hear me, Sylvia? Nigel has remembered what happened."

Constance's indrawn breath was the only sound in the garden. Elisande held her own breath as she waited for Sylvia's reaction. It was not long in coming.

"So then he must *know* he is innocent. Why should he go away because of *that*?" Sylvia wailed. "Unless—oh God, he *cannot* have done all those awful things?"

The girl was either an excellent actress or telling the truth—she really knew nothing. "What if he did sell those secrets to the French?" Elisande demanded.

"You mean if he—oh, I don't care," Sylvia cried passionately. "I don't care what he's done or not done. I *love* Nigel. I'm going to go with you to Sussex."

"Oh, no you won't," said Constance sternly.

Elisande added, "It's not so simple. You see, he *remembers* about the golden Spanish combs."

Once more she searched Sylvia's face. "Combs?" Sylvia asked petulantly. "I don't know what is so important about those plaguey combs. I told you I only wore them until the first dance. They were so heavy they gave me a headache, so I took them off."

"I don't believe you," Constance said bluntly. "You wore them when you went out to the Cliff Path—"

"Con! Remember, you promised!"

At Elisande's warning cry, Constance blushed a

hot magenta and turned away. Meanwhile, Sylvia was exclaiming, "The Cliff Path? You must be joking, or else you are as mad as a March hare. I most certainly did not go out at all."

"Then did you take the combs off and go back to the dancing?" Elisande queried.

"No. I told you before—I had the headache. I went and lay down and fell asleep, and when I woke up, they'd found Nigel—" Sylvia broke off to call her abigail, who was standing some distance away. "Whitton will tell you, if you don't believe me."

The woman came forward and dropped a curtsy. "That awful night, ma'am? I'll remember it till I die, indeed to God. You had the headache and Mrs. Hanard—she was Lady Graymount then—helped you upstairs. Her and me, we took off those heavy combs. Lady Graymount said that it was the combs' weight that gave you the headache."

As the girl spoke, something insistent that had been nudging against Elisande's brain clicked into place. Everything suddenly made sense. "Did Anabelle stay with you for some time, Sylvia?" she asked.

The girl shook her head. "Only for a few moments. Then she told Whitton to bathe my head with lavender water. Oh—and she offered to put the combs away for me. She was most obliging."

Most obliging indeed. "It makes sense," Elisande murmured. "Of course. She took the combs and wore them herself."

"She? Who is 'she'?" Constance asked, baffled. "What are you talking about?"

Sylvia was looking bewildered, too, but to Elisande it was perfectly clear. " 'Things are not as they seem,' " she quoted softly. "Con, don't you see? The woman Nigel followed down to Swan's Cove that night was not Sylvia at all. It was—"

There was a rustle of silk and taffeta, a drift of expensive perfume. "Are you waiting for me, my dears?" called a silvery voice.

Chapter Eleven

"What is all this about Spanish combs?" Anabelle Hanard was asking. Gliding gracefully into the garden, she struck an attitude and announced, "Rejoice with me, my dears—my run of bad luck is finally over. At Mrs. Dinrail's breakfast gathering today, I trounced Lady Carme at piquet."

She nodded to Sylvia's abigail, who waited just out of earshot, and called, "Whitton—go back to the house and ask cook to lay out refreshments in the blue room. The ladies will join me in celebrating my triumph."

"I am afraid we cannot stay," Elisande demurred. "We are on our way to Sussex and have called only to say good-bye."

She thought that she had seldom seen the colonel's lady in such high spirits or looking so well. She was dressed in a sapphire blue merino walking-out dress with close-fitting long sleeves and a daringly low décolletage. A hat decorated with flowers and leaves tilted jauntily low across her forehead, and small blue kid boots peered from beneath her ankle-length skirts.

Her eyes were merry and as kind as they had always been, and Elisande's newfound suspicions fell into disarray. Was it possible she had been mistaken?

"So you are really going back to Sussex. How sad

it is that you are going home with nothing accomplished."

"Not quite nothing," Constance said in her gruffest voice. "Nigel has remembered everything about that night."

She stared hard at Sylvia as she spoke, but it was Anabelle Hanard who exclaimed sharply, "What do you mean? Remembered what?"

"Lord Raven brought a mesmerist from France to help Nigel remember what took place on March thirtieth," Elisande explained.

"A *what*? Lud, my dear, you surely cannot believe such foolishness. I am shocked that Raven would be party to such a smoky affair."

Anabelle gave the gold reticule she held a little swing, as Elisande continued, "Mme Benoit took Nigel back to the night of March thirtieth. And he *did* remember, Anabelle. He told us everything that happened that night."

For an instant, fear and dismay flashed in Anabelle's blue eyes, and Elisande's heart bumped painfully. *No*, she thought, *I wasn't mistaken.*

Aloud she pressed on, "Nigel remembered going to the study where he discovered that the dispatches were gone. He tried to find the colonel, who was nowhere to be found. Then he went into the garden where he saw a lady hurrying down the Cliff Path."

Constance was plucking at her sleeve. "You promised to say nothing, Elisande," she whispered urgently.

Ignoring her cousin, Elisande continued, "This lady wore Spanish combs in her hair."

Sylvia looked bewildered, but Anabelle cried merrily, "Can it be that it was our Sylvia that your brother saw? Lud, but it is a romance we are listening to and vastly entertaining. Do go on, my dear. What happened next?"

"Nigel followed the lady down to Swan's Cove. Here she met a French agent."

"Oh lud, what is this you say? I cannot credit that my own stepdaughter was the traitress all this time."

As Anabelle cried out in horror, Sylvia Hanard protested in even more horrified tones, "But—but that can't be! I never went on the Cliff Path or anywhere else that night. I tell you, I was lying down with the headache. Nigel mistook someone else for me." She turned pleadingly to Constance, who turned her back. "Elisande, Stepmama—you surely don't think that I—"

"Unfeeling child," Anabelle moaned. She put a hand on her white bosom as if to quiet it. "This is beyond everything. Sylvia—you said you loved Mr. Redding, yet you left him in hell this long time. Now, at last, he has remembered."

"Yes," Elisande said quietly, "Nigel remembers it all. But it wasn't Sylvia that he saw. You were the lady with the Spanish combs, Anabelle."

There was a gasp from Constance, and Sylvia's eyes became as large as saucers. "I think you have gone mad," Anabelle said angrily. "Too many cares on your young shoulders have brought on brain fever."

She half turned to go toward the house, but Sylvia jumped up from her garden seat and cried, "But—but it *could* have been you, Stepmama. You were the one who took off my combs—and then you told Whitton not to bother putting them away, because you would do it."

"Anabelle didn't put the combs away," Elisande interposed. "She wore them when she went to the colonel's study and stole those dispatches."

"Tol rol," snapped Anabelle. Her eyes had narrowed to blue slits, and there were red spots burning high on her cheekbones. "And how was I supposed to get into the locked safe, pray? I supposed I snapped my fingers and summoned a genie to aid me?"

"When they had put the dispatches in the safe, Nigel said that he and the colonel met you in the hall. I think you were spying on them and discovered where the spare key was kept."

Anabelle saw that Sylvia and Constance were staring at her aghast. She glared at Elisande and spat, "So now I listen at keyholes, do I? You haven't gone mad—you are drunk. To think that I could betray my own husband—"

"He was not your husband then," Elisande interrupted. "You were a young widow, alone in the world. As you told me once, your life was a hard one." Though her heart was beating wildly, she managed to keep her voice steady. "You had no money, and no offers of marriage, and you were desperate."

"The Knight of Pentacles," Constance said suddenly. "The cards have been right all along. They *told* me that a fair-haired person wasn't to be trusted. I thought they were warning me about Lord Raven, but all the time the cards meant Mrs. Hanard."

"The cards—it all comes down to the cards, doesn't it?" Anabelle mused. Almost in friendly fashion she added, "You were quite clever to unravel the Gordian knot, Elisande. But you don't know the whole story. Shall I tell it?"

Without waiting for an answer, the colonel's lady began, "I have always liked games of chance. My late father, Lord Hatton, used to say that it was in the blood. *He* lost his inheritance, you know, so that I was forced to marry Graymount." She made a face. "He was a starched-up old squeeze-crab, three times my age, and he kept the screws on me, but even so I gamed when I could. And after he died, I cut loose—and lost all of Graymount's money, alas. Especially I lost to a Mr. George Fensby."

The colonel's wife explained that Mr. Fensby had then revealed himself as a French agent. "He knew that Colonel Hanard was one of my admirers. He also believed that Wellington would soon be sending the colonel dispatches crucial to the French. So, in return for forgetting my debt, Fensby told me to steal those dispatches."

Calmly she added, "You see, it was a matter of survival. I had no choice but to agree."

" 'He will find out the truth—and he will not find out the truth.' " Wide-eyed, Constance exclaimed, "The cards were right again. Anyone seeing Lady Anabelle Graymount coming out of the colonel's study would have thought she was Sylvia—as Nigel did."

"I regret that." Oddly enough, Anabelle sounded sincere as she added, "I truly liked Captain Redding and was sorry to see him in such straits."

"Sorry?" Sylvia shrieked. She had been listening in mute horror but now, like a fury, she launched herself at her stepmother. "You ruined his life—and mine—and all for your filthy gambling. I will scratch out your eyes!"

Elisande caught hold of Sylvia's shoulders and managed to hold her back. "Anabelle, did you order those villains to beat Nigel to death?"

The colonel's lady snapped open her reticule, took out a handkerchief, and blew her little nose. "That really wasn't my idea. Fensby felt that since Captain Redding had seen us both, he should die. But the fools botched their work, and the young man lived. Luckily, he had no memory of what had happened. Because he couldn't incriminate me, I was willing to let sleeping dogs die."

"How noble of you!"

Anabelle rolled her eyes impatiently. "Oh, lud,

Elisande, you are a sensible woman. I pray you will consider my alternatives. If Captain Redding had remembered what really happened that night, his testimony would have cost me my life."

And when the Reddings had come to Dorset, Anabelle had become alarmed. She had befriended them because she needed to know how much Nigel did remember. "When you were afraid that his memory was returning, you hired ruffians to ambush Nigel and me," Elisande accused. "Only, Lord Raven was there."

Unconcernedly Anabelle returned her handkerchief to her reticule. "Lord Raven," she pointed out, "Is not here now."

Afternoon sunlight winked on the barrel of a small pistol she had withdrawn from her reticule. "I don't want to hurt you," she said, "but you can see that there is nothing else I can do. I can't allow you to go away knowing all that you know."

"By all means shoot us," Elisande snapped. "Someone from the house will hear the noise."

"You are wrong." As swift as a snake, Anabelle turned on Constance, who was standing closest to her. Taken by surprise, Constance had no time to struggle before Anabelle's arm was locked tightly around her neck.

"No noise," Anabelle warned coolly. "Now, we are all going for a walk. Do not make a fuss, ladies, or I will be forced to shoot poor Miss Dayton through the head."

Sylvia began to curse her stepmother. Elisande gazed distractedly at Constance, whose face was turning red from the pressure of Anabelle's arm. "Don't hurt my cousin," she begged. "I'll do anything you say."

Anabelle gestured with her pistol, indicating that they were to walk up the Cliff Path. As Elisande hesitated, Sylvia whispered, "There are two of us. We can overpower her."

Elisande shook her head. "I can't endanger Con's life."

"No talking," Anabelle ordered sharply. "Commence walking, ladies, or I blow off Miss Dayton's head."

It seemed to Elisande that her knees had gone weak and that her legs could no longer bear her weight. *Fool*, she called herself bitterly, idiot for accusing Anabelle Hanard to her face—bird-wit for having played into her hands. Now they would all die and Nigel would never know that the treacherous lady in the shadows had not been Sylvia.

She tried to think of some way of escape as they traversed a long, looping path that trailed between groves of oak and pine, but her thoughts skittered like beads of water over glass. All she could think was that she was retracing the steps Nigel had taken that night.

The sounds of the sea grew progressively louder, and soon they stepped off the path onto a clearing. At the end of the clearing was a jumble of rocks, which the colonel's wife indicated with her pistol.

"You will walk to the edge of those rocks," she ordered. "How sad it will be when it's learned that the three of you had an accident. Sylvia was showing you the cliff walk when the ground gave way beneath you and the three of you fell to your deaths."

"Help!" Sylvia shouted, but her voice was lost in the noise of the surf below. "Oh, you bloody, murdering, horrible *bitch*!"

Anabelle's laugh was no longer silvery. "Sticks and stones don't break bones, my charming stepdaughter. Rocks, on the other hand—"

She broke off as Elisande stared hard at a point

behind her. "Ivo!" she cried. "Thank God you are here!"

Anabelle automatically glanced over her shoulder. Elisande lunged forward and seized the pistol. She was strong, but so was Anabelle, and the two women struggled for the weapon.

"*Now*, you witch!"

Sylvia hurled herself on Anabelle who fell, taking Sylvia and Elisande with her. The pistol skittered out of her hand, and Elisande seized it. "Now we have *you*," Sylvia exulted.

"Let 'er go."

Elisande whipped around at the familiar, raspy voice. Behind them stood a hulking, hairy individual with a prominent gold tooth and a wicked face that Elisande remembered only too well. He gestured with the pistol he held in his hand as he added, "I said, let 'er leddyship go."

Reluctantly Elisande let the pistol fall. "That's better. Come on up, you lot."

Four other ruffians made their appearance from behind a jumble of rocks at the cliffs' edge. "Now the shoe's on the other foot, hain't it?" Gold Tooth was asking gleefully. "You got away from me an' the boys once before, missy, but you hain't going to do it again. This time Ned 'Ackett 'as got you where 'e wants you."

"I say, Ivo—it'll be good to be back home."

The marquess eased his rump onto a more comfortable spot in the curricle and leaned back as if he had not a care in the world. "Deuced jolly, seein' the dear old place again," he went on. "Tanner Place—best home in the whole world. I was mad to leave it. Shan't leave it again for anythin'."

Wordlessly Lord Raven ground his teeth. For the past hour he had endured in silence while his brother extolled the virtues of his estate and his pleasure at going home.

"Suppose you must be thinkin' of the sea, Ivo," the marquess continued. "Deuced jolly place, the sea must be. Not that I ever want to travel on it—crossed the channel once, and that was enough for me. I say, won't it be jolly seein' Tanner Place again?"

"Wigram," Lord Raven declared, "if you don't stop nattering, I will strangle you and leave your body in a ditch."

"Oh, I say," bleated the marquess. Indignantly he added, "Fine thing when a chap can't even talk about goin' home in peace. What's makin' you look so black and fly into the ropes, old fellow? Open your budget, that's the ticket. Not happy to be goin' back to the sea?"

"I don't want to hear about the sea either," Lord Raven snarled.

The marquess muttered, "I say," under his breath several times and fell into a brown study. "Ivo," he finally exclaimed, "you're right as usual. Mean to say—I'm not happy about goin' home, neither."

Lord Raven begged to know what new maggot had invaded his brother's feeble brain. "Ain't a new maggot. Old one," the marquess protested. A familiar, mulish look hardened his chubby features as he added, "Fact is that I can't stomach the idea of going off without so much as sayin' good-bye to Miss Dayton."

In several terse sentences, Lord Raven consigned his brother to Hades. But, the fair-minded part of him argued, it was not all Wigram's fault. Though hardly a mental giant, Wigram had put his finger on the pulse of things, for he himself had not even been thinking of the sea. He had been remembering Elisande Redding.

And not just the feel of her in his arms, or the taste of her lips—all of which could have been reasoned away as part of an infatuation that would later mellow into vague but pleasant memories. The problem, Raven thought, was that he missed *her*, Elisande. The way she turned her head slightly to the side when she was perplexed. The way her eyes darkened when she was thoughtful. Her laughter. Her wide-eyed wonder that day when the swans came sailing over the sea.

"Damnation," Lord Raven swore. The marquess cast a worried glance at him but forbore to comment. "Confusion take it—I don't have time for a woman in my life."

Nor had he. His life was full of adventure and enjoyment. To him happiness was fine sailing weather and a new moon at sea, or the sight of an unknown horizon with all its secrets intact and its treasures yet to discover. He would have become stifled in Dorset, or Sussex, or Kent, or any such boring spot. That was why he was leaving—had to leave.

Lord Raven tried to conjure up a moonrise in the New World but instead of that fabulous sight, found himself recalling the afternoon when he had seen Elisande last. He recalled every nuance of her profile, the scent of her, the fact that if he had reached out he could have drawn her into his arms. Yet he had not done so.

"There was a reason," he said aloud. "There really is a reason for this."

"Yes, that's right, a reason." The marquess's eager voice interrupted his thoughts, and Raven realized that his brother had been jabbering away for some time. "You understand, don't you? Mean to say—how'd it look, goin' off with her book? Miss Dayton'd think I had no manners."

Lord Raven attempted to focus on what the man

was saying. "You mean you've got a book that belongs to Miss Dayton?" he finally asked.

The marquess nodded eagerly. "That's it—I say, that's it exactly, Ivo. Always knew you were a downy one. Miss Dayton lent me this book on beekeepin'. Forgot about it till this moment, give you my word. Not the act of a gentleman, lopin' off with that deuced book, Ivo. Not done at all."

Lord Raven opened his mouth to say that his brother could always send the book to Miss Dayton, but the words never came. Instead, he called sharply to his grays.

"My lord? My lord!" shrilled Landers as Lord Raven's curricle shot past the valets' lumbering carriage. "Your lordship, where are—? What has—? Oh, I do believe that Lord Raven has gone entirely mad. He is driving the wrong way."

With Landers's distressed cries ringing in his ears, Lord Raven urged his grays back along the road they had traveled. "I hope you know," he shouted at his brother, "that your valet isn't going to speak to you in a week."

"Bother Landers," the marquess yelled back happily. Then he added in great trepidation, "Ivo, aren't we goin' d-deucedly fast, old fellow? Ain't complainin', mind you, but seems to me, it'd be b-better if we arrive in one piece."

With unabated speed but with consummate skill, Lord Raven drove back into Camston-on-Sea. He was on watch for every trap and carriage that passed them on the road, but he saw no sign of the Reddings. But when they rattled down the road toward Willoughby Cottage, no carriage stood at the door.

The marquess gave a groan. "Too late," he exclaimed.

Lord Raven felt a sudden and sharp jab in the vicinity of his heart. "So it seems," he said dryly. "I should have guessed this was a fool's errand. It's made us late and we'll need to make haste to— what the devil are you doing now?"

The marquess was scrambling down from the curricle. "Didn't see them passin' us on the road. Maybe someone knows which way they went."

As he spoke, they heard male voices arguing nearby, and a loud Yorkshire voice expostulated, "Nay, Captain, 'twas not my fault, any road. I'm mithered as th'art, think on. I did not see t'ladies leaving—nor do I know where they went."

Around the corner of the cottage came Parse and Nigel Redding, who was demanding heatedly, "Hell and the devil, Parse, where could they have got to?"

He broke off as he saw Lord Raven and the marquess. "I thought you were on the road to Scotland," he exclaimed.

"Miss Dayton's not here?" the marquess blurted before his brother had a chance to speak. "Must be around somewhere since you're here. Mean to say, the ladies can't have gone back to Sussex on their own."

Nigel looked both annoyed and perplexed. "Don't ask me where they are," he growled. "Here we're all set to leave—all packed up and prepared to go— only to find that the women have gone off someplace in the hired trap."

There was a diffident little cough from the near distance. "If I may, sir—"

Dressed in her habitual black, Mrs. Willoughby was walking toward them. "We come just to say good-bye, sir," she said. "Seeing as no one 'as come to say good-bye, me and 'Arriet 'ave come to do the friendly thing," she explained.

She cast a reproachful eye in Parse's direction. The Yorkshireman visibly quailed as Mrs. Willoughby repeated bitterly, "I say the *friendly* thing to do, seeing as 'ow we're neighbors, and seeing as 'ow my little girl took so much pleasure and delight from your company, Mr. Parse—"

"Stow it, Ma," Harriet interrupted crisply. "Mr. Parse ain't going to be turned up sweet by any o' that. 'E don't fancy marrying you, and that's that."

The widow blushed scarlet and hissed that she was going to box her daughter's ears. Harriet merely rolled her eyes. She might be dressed like a girl, Lord Raven thought, amused, but her character had hardly changed.

He asked whether they had seen Miss Redding or Miss Dayton, and to his relief, Harriet nodded. "They passed Ma an' me on their way to 'Anard 'Ouse an hour since."

"To Hanard House!" Nigel echoed, flushing up, and Lord Raven said thoughtfully that the ladies had been gone a long time. "Perhaps there's trouble," Nigel then said. "I'm riding out there with you, Raven."

"Not on this curricle, you ain't." The marquess scrambled back onto the curricle announcing, "I'm deuced goin', too."

"Nay, an' th'aren't going without me," Parse exclaimed. "Not this time, Captain."

At this moment the carriage containing the valets and the luggage came rattling into view. Behind it trotted the spare horses. "Perkins, unharness two of those horses," Lord Raven commanded his groom.

He drew a serviceable pistol from his belt adding, "I always go armed during a journey overland. Do you arm yourself, too, Nigel, and come up behind us. Parse, you and Perkins will follow on horseback."

Whipping up the horses, he started down the road toward Hanard House. "Lisa swore to me that she wouldn't tell Sylvia anything about— anything," Nigel shouted against the wind. "Why would she have gone to Hanard House?"

Lord Raven's only response was to urge his grays

still faster. "Sorry, Wigram, but we must go swiftly," he called.

"Don't signify," panted the marquess resolutely. "Miss Dayton may be in danger—g-go fast as you like, dear old fellow."

Fifteen minutes later, they were clattering up to Hanard House. "Still here, on my life—there's the trap they were driving," Nigel exclaimed.

The heavy front door now banged open and Colonel Hanard appeared on the steps. His welcoming expression changed almost immediately to a scowl as he recognized the occupants of the curricle.

"I thought," he said haughtily, "that whatever association we have had is over."

"I say, never mind about that," shouted the marquess urgently. "Where's Miss Dayton gone to?"

Ignoring the marquess, Colonel Hanard growled, "Redding, I told you never to set foot on my property."

Lord Raven spoke quickly to forestall a confrontation. "We've come in search of Miss Redding and her cousin," he explained. "They drove out here more than an hour ago, and we are concerned that they may have come to some harm."

"That's their vehicle," Nigel added tersely. "Where are they?"

"I have no idea," the colonel snapped back angrily. Then, compelled by Raven's steady gaze, he added unwillingly, "They may be with my daughter."

"Oh, I say, I don't like the sound of *that*," the marquess muttered. "No tellin' what she might do."

"And where is Mrs. Hanard?" Lord Raven went on.

The colonel scowled and muttered something about damnable impertinence. "I have no idea," he replied curtly. "I have just now returned from riding, so I have no notion where she's gone to. Eh? The servants say she returned from breakfasting with Mrs. Dinrail, but she's not in the house or the garden. Perhaps she's taking a walk with the other women."

As he spoke there was the sound of hoofbeats approaching and Perkins, followed by Parse, rode up on the spare horses. "We've come by a short cut through the woods, my lord," Raven's groom reported. "As we climbed the hill we could see there's a vessel in Swan's Cove."

"The *Silver Raven's* returned?" Lord Raven asked astonished, and his man shook his head.

"No, my lord, not the *Raven*. This one was a square, ugly little tub of a boat—the kind that's only good for running across the channel."

"A ship—now that bears investigating," the colonel exclaimed. "Eh? Perhaps Mrs. Hanard and the women went down to Swan's Cove to look at this ship. I'll take the smuggler's road down to the cove and see if they're there."

"Take these men with you," Lord Raven urged. "The rest of us will follow the Cliff Path."

The colonel stalked off followed by Parse and Perkins while the other two men hastened toward the garden. "I say, Ivo, wait for me," the marquess entreated.

The marquess puffed in their wake until he reached a narrow, winding path that led from the garden into the trees. Here he stopped dead in his tracks. "Deuce take it—there's her cards!" he exclaimed.

With considerable difficulty he bent down and plucked up something from the grass. "Here's one of Constance's—I mean, Miss Dayton's—tarot cards," he puffed.

Lord Raven called from further down the path.

"Here's another. Apparently Miss Dayton has left us a trail to follow."

"Clever Constance!" But the marquess was talking to himself for Lord Raven and Nigel were already out of sight. "Knew there'd be trouble," the little marquess muttered. Then, determinedly clasping his walking stick, he plunged after the others.

Chapter Twelve

The gold-toothed Ned Hackett extended a grimy hand to help Anabelle Hanard regain her feet. "Wot does yer want us to do with these 'ere morts?" he asked.

Gone was Anabelle's air of charming grace. Strands of her hair floated untidily around her head, the shoulder of her dress had been torn, and there was dirt on her cheek. Her eyes were as hard as chips of blue ice.

"First things first," she said in a voice that was harsh and ugly. "Where did you and your henchmen spring from? I told you never to come near the house."

"Well, we 'aven't been paid for the last time, 'ave we?" Ned retorted heatedly. "The boys and me wants wot you owes us."

"You may *want* all you like." The colonel's wife tapped her small foot impatiently. "If you recall the *last* time you made such a mull of things that you did not deserve payment."

"That ain't 'ow *we* sees it," retorted Ned combatively. "Look 'ere, me leddy, 'ere's the lay. Hengland is getting a leetle warm for the boys and me, so we're getting ready to 'op the twig across the channel. Some mates of our'n are waiting for us in the cove right now, but afore we go we wants some rolls of soft to make the trip easier."

As a murmur of agreement rose from the waiting

villains, Elisande's flagging hopes revived. "There is no way she's going to pay you," she cried. "She has no money."

Anabelle Hanard darted forth and slapped Elisande hard across the mouth. "Be silent, you lying bitch," she snarled. Then she added, "Of course I'll pay you, you fools. I have the money back at the house."

Seeing that Ned looked unconvinced, Elisande added coals to the fire. "Mrs. Hanard is a gambler. She herself admitted that it was in her blood. People like that never have any money."

Sylvia immediately nodded. "That's right. She even tried to borrow money from *me* because she was in dun territory." She added in an insinuating voice, "She doesn't have any money, but *I* do. If you let us go, I'll give you enough gold to make you rich."

Ned scowled. His henchmen eyed each other and sucked their teeth. "I thinks we'll wait until you pass us some rolls of soft afore we toss these gentry morts over the rocks," he said at last. "I dunno as you're trying to slumguzzle us, yer leddyship, but I'm a peevy cove. Better safe'n sorry, I allus says."

"Could be the red'eaded mort 'as a lot o' brass," one of his henchmen added. "Could be we oughter do as she says."

"Idiots!" Anabelle shrieked. "What is the matter with you all? These women have seen you and heard everything you said. They can point you out to the law, and you'll hang."

"And if you believe *her*, you'll never be paid," Elisande flung back. "She can betray you to the law and you'll hang anyway."

Ned looked nervous. "This 'ere is a queer fetch," he growled. "Wot're you saying?"

"She's saying that you'd be short a sheet to trust Stepmama," Sylvia snapped. "Have you got bats in your upper works? She doesn't want to pay you, so she'll go to the law and inform on you. There's no honor amongst thieves—"

She broke off as her stepmother lunged forward and snatched the pearls that hung around her neck.

"Here," she snarled. "Take these. They're worth many times over what I agreed to pay you for killing the Reddings—which is more than you lummoxes deserve. Now, throw these women over the cliffs. See if you can do something properly for once."

Frowning, Ned held the pearls up to the light. "They're false," Sylvia said promptly. "They're paste, worth nothing. Papa had to sell all my jewelry because his charming wife gambled everything away."

"Then you ain't got no brass neither. Trying to slumguzzle me, was you?" Ned flung down the pearls and barked. "All right, boys. 'Eave them over the side. I'll do this 'un myself."

"We don't have any money," Elisande cried desperately, as Ned seized her around the waist, "but Lord Raven does. He has a great deal of money, and he will pay for our safe return."

Her words were received with roars of laughter. "Garn," Ned snickered. "Yer think so, do yer? Yer don't know much about the gentry, gal, an' that's a fact. That there Lord Raven was just 'aving some fun wit'yer, 'ats all. 'E wouldn't pay a guinea fer yer. Besides, we seen 'is nibs' curricle ride orf from the Gilded Stag hours since."

Elisande felt the bitterness of despair. It had been their last chance. No use to strive or fight any longer—but then she heard Constance crying as she struggled with the grinning brute who was dragging her toward the rocks.

Con had come to Hanard House only because of

her, and now she was going to die. "I'm sorry," Elisande called out to her cousin as they were dragged toward the cliffs. "This is all my fault."

"No, it isn't." In spite of her tears, Constance sounded resolute. "I came with you of my own free will, and I'm glad we discovered that the traitor wasn't Sylvia. I think," she added earnestly to the colonel's daughter, "you are very pretty and brave, and I am sorry I called you a heartless minx."

Anabelle began to laugh. "You are a monster," Sylvia panted. "All this time you pretended to like me."

"I don't *dis*like any of you." In a parody of her old elegant manner, Anabelle added, "Lud, I regret doing this. But, you see, if I don't kill you, it will become awkward. After all, you know who sold those dispatches to the French, and I should be forced to fly to the continent like Ned Hackett and his friends. And that would not suit me at all."

She nodded to her henchmen. "For God's sake," she snapped, "get it over with."

Suddenly Elisande uttered a glad cry. "Ivo," she gasped. "Oh, Ivo, you're *here!*"

Anabelle Hanard looked pained. "If you think you're going to entrap me with that same old snare—"

Before she could complete her sentence, she was shoved roughly aside. Next moment, Ned screamed as powerful hands seized him by the throat and flung him backward, away from Elisande. There was a dull thud as he hit his head on a rock, after which he gave a wheeze and lay still.

"Ivo," Elisande repeated joyfully.

Lord Raven reached out and pulled her into his arms, and she clung to him. He had come—he had come after all. Elisande's heart swelled with triumph and joy. She did not question why or how

Lord Raven had appeared in the nick of time. All that mattered was that he was there.

There was sharp, cracking noises, and a bullet buried itself in the ground at their feet. Lord Raven pushed Elisande behind some rocks and cautioned, "Stay down."

"But Con needs help—and Sylvia, too. She is *not* the traitress we supposed her to be," Elisande said urgently.

She broke off as she heard Nigel's shout and, looking out from behind the protective rock, saw that her brother was at Sylvia's side. He was grappling with two of the ruffians.

"They're too close to him—I don't want to risk a shot," Lord Raven said. He replaced the pistol he had drawn in his belt and added tersely, "Stay *down*, I said."

Before Elisande could protest, he was gone. But before he could reach the struggling Nigel, a woman's scream rent the air.

"Con!" Elisande gasped. "Con, where are you?"

As if in answer, there was another shriek and, to her horror, Elisande saw Constance standing on the edge of the cliffs. One of the villains was pointing a pistol at her.

"Let her be, you beast!" Elisande shouted. She started to run toward her cousin, then screamed a protest as the big brute reached out and grasped Con's shoulder.

"Halt! I say, halt, you swine!"

The ruffian half turned at the wheezing shout, and next moment Wigram, Marquess Tanner, came puffing onto the scene. "I'm comin'," panted the marquess. "I'm comin', my—my dear! Take *that*, you deuced scoundrel!"

Swinging his walking stick above his head, he aimed a blow at Constance's attacker but tripped over a stone and sprawled at the villain's feet.

The grinning ruffian let go of Constance and aimed his pistol at the marquess. But before he could fire, Constance pushed him from behind with all her strength. Simultaneously, the marquess grabbed the ruffian by the leg and yanked forward. As the man fell, Constance lunged after his pistol and caught it in midair.

"Don't you m-move," she stuttered. "If you take a st-step, I will sh-shoot."

Dizzy with thanksgiving, Elisande started to cross over to them but stopped as she saw a flash of blue. Looking up, she saw Anabelle Hanard hurrying away around the rocks and down the cliff.

Anabelle was getting away in the confusion. No one else was paying attention. Lord Raven and Nigel were busy subduing the two ruffians, and Constance and the marquess had their hands full. No one but Elisande had seen the colonel's wife.

Swiftly she followed Anabelle around the rocks then stopped at the top of a narrow stairway hewn into the side of the cliff. From this vantage point Elisande could see the full sweep of Swan's Cove and the dirty white sail of a squat, square boat bobbing close to the pier.

The steps were narrow and uneven, the trail downward steep and perilous—Elisande hesitated. She knew she should call for help, but there was no time. As if hell itself were nipping at her heels, the colonel's wife was scrambling down the steps. As she heard Elisande following her, she whipped around to show a face distorted with fear and rage.

"Don't come near me," she panted. "Get away from me."

Sunlight blazed for a second on the pistol in Anabelle's hand, then there was a sharp report and almost simultaneously a searing pain.

As Elisande cried out, Anabelle Hanard tore

down the steps toward the beach. "Keep *away* from me!" she shouted over her shoulder.

Ignoring the warmth that was trickling down her arm, Elisande followed the other woman. She could not let Anabelle get away. She must be made to confess, to give evidence that would not only clear Nigel's name but Sylvia's as well—

"*C'me'ere*, you!" Ned, wild eyed and with a large bump on his head, had suddenly appeared from behind a tangle of trees and rocks. "Now this is all bowman! You're me ticket out o' this mess," he grated.

Elisande tried to avoid his grasping hands, but desperation had made Ned nimble. She screamed in pain as he caught her wounded arm and twisted it behind her back.

"Now we're going to go down to the beach, nice and slow," he snarled in her ear. "See that boat? Us are going down and getting into it. Yer mates won't try ter stop me if yer with me."

There was the sound of a shot. Ned screamed and let go of Elisande yelling, "Me arm! Me arm's 'it!"

Still bellowing, he raced down the steps towards the beach below. "I thought I told you to stay behind that rock," Lord Raven called from the steps above.

"They're getting away" was all Elisande could think of to say. "Ned Hackett and Anabelle are escaping."

"They're not going anywhere. The colonel, Parse, and Perkins are down at the cove." Hurrying down the steps, Lord Raven demanded, "Did he hurt you?"

Mutely she shook her head. "The others?"

"The scoundrels have been all captured, and Nigel recognized them as the same ones who attacked you the other night." Lord Raven replaced his pistol in his belt as he added, "Hanard's servants arrived on the scene in time to take the unsavory lot away. The law has been summoned, and—good God, what's this? You *are* hurt."

"It's nothing," Elisande tried to say stoutly, but she had begun to feel a little sick. "I—I am perfectly all right."

"The hell you are." Lord Raven gritted. He pulled up her sleeve and examined the cut. "Clean," he said in terse relief, "and not deep. But you've lost some blood. Here—sit down here on this rock."

"But are you sure Anabelle is not getting away?" Elisande protested. The weakness in her legs had returned, and she sank down on the stone as Lord Raven tore off his cravat and used it as a bandage.

"Certain," Lord Raven said. "Let Hanard see to his wife, sweetheart, and let me take care of you."

The dizziness she now felt had nothing to do with the wound. "*What* did you call me?" Elisande whispered.

Lord Raven's skilled fingers bound the wound tight. Then his eyes met hers, steady and even. "It seems to be what I've been calling you in my heart," he said. "Do you dislike it, Elisande?"

She had barely time to shake her head before he had gathered her into his arms and was kissing her with a concentrated passion that took away all other thought.

The pain in Elisande's arm vanished. Her faintness disappeared, and she felt strong and vigorous. In fact, she had never felt better or more alive in all her days. For the space of time in which their lips clung together, the world turned golden, the sun shone warm as summer, and there was no sound but the beating of their hearts.

The need to breathe drove them finally apart, and they looked at each other somewhat dazedly.

"I thought," she managed to gasp, "that you

were going back to the New World and new adventures. I thought you could not leave Dorset quickly enough."

"I thought so, too." Lord Raven's voice was husky, and his mouth curved almost softly as he added, "It seems that I was wrong."

He kissed her again, more passionately than he had done before, so that dark spots danced before Elisande's eyes even when they finally drew apart. Perhaps those spots interfered with her usually clear-sighted vision, because she did not ask herself logical questions about the unsuitability of falling in love with a man of the world. Instead she drew a deep, happy sigh and rested her cheek against Lord Raven's shoulder.

"I should never have gone," he was saying. "I'm an idiot not to have realized that sooner. Even Wigram had more sense."

As Lord Raven spoke, they heard voices, muted by the sound of the surf, rising from the beach below. Though she could not clearly make out the words, Elisande could hear the pain in the colonel's voice, and the thought of his agony at his wife's disgrace made her sick at heart.

Lord Raven seemed to sense her thought. "Let's go up," he said. He helped her to her feet and going before her, drew her up the steps after him. "Why do you say that the marquess has more sense than you?" Elisande called up to him.

"He didn't want to leave Dorset without saying good-bye to your cousin. And he saw through my pretenses, too. Sweetheart, I can't promise that life with me will be easy—"

He was interrupted by a gasp from Elisande. "Ivo—do you tell me that your brother has a *tendre* for Con?"

Before Lord Raven could answer, there was the sound of someone clearing his throat up above.

"You're a brave woman, my dear—Miss Dayton, I mean," the marquess was heard to declare. "You saved my life. I say, if you hadn't hit that deuced scoundrel back there, I'd have been singin' deuced psalms by now."

Lord Raven helped Elisande up onto the cliff top just in time to see Constance and the marquess walking slowly away. They were arm in arm, and they were walking so close that their shoulders bumped together.

"I was not in the least bit brave," Constance was protesting.

"Yes, you are. And clever, too. Imagine havin' the presence of mind to leave a trail of your tarot cards behind so we could find and rescue you! Those cards are deuced useful, that's what I say. Seem to know what they're talkin' about, too. Must give me a, whatchumaycall it—a—a readin' sometime."

Elisande was amazed to see her cousin shake her head. "I will do so if you wish, but the cards are only bits of paper and paint and cannot really foretell anything. They have helped me pass the time but—oh, Wigram—I mean, my lord—you were so *brave* to come to my rescue as you did. So *heroic*."

"I say, was I really?" The marquess seemed stunned at the idea. "Never thought meself brave, y'know," he added humbly. "Not much in m'brainbox, neither. But, mean to say—I'd walk through fire for you, my—my dear Constance."

"If I know anything at all," Lord Raven mused, as he and Elisande watched the couple stroll blissfully off together. "Wigram will be declaring himself within ten minutes."

Elisande drew a happy sigh. "They will suit *so* well, and they will have a wondrously peaceful life together raising bees and piglets and growing herbs for Con's teas. I can't imagine any two people who will be more content."

" 'Content,' " Lord Raven repeated. His dark face turned thoughtful as he added, "Is that what you want from life, Elisande?"

"But you could not have believed that of me! How dare you think that I could be capable of such a dishonorable act?"

The passionate words emanated from the near distance. "What Cheltenham tragedy is about to befall us now?" Lord Raven wanted to know.

Sylvia Hanard had come stalking out from behind a large rock. Her disheveled red hair streamed behind her like a flag in battle, and her emerald eyes snapped fire. "To *think* that I cried myself to sleep every day for a year while you considered me a mean, conniving, horrible *bitch*!"

Nigel, who had followed her from behind the rock, was protesting, "I never said I believed you were a traitress."

"Traitress! As if I cared about *that*," Sylvia shouted. "What I can't abide is that you believed that I could order those beasts to beat you to death. And—and how could you *possibly* think that I would be so despicable as to let you carry the blame all this time?"

"I couldn't. On my life, Sylvia, that's why I blocked out what I saw—*thought* I saw, I mean—and lost my memory."

"I hate you!"

Whirling on her heel, Sylvia started striding away toward the Cliff Path. Before she could reach it, however, Nigel caught her by the shoulders and jerked her around to face him.

"I was never going to reveal what I'd remembered. I wanted to protect you even when I thought you had taken those papers."

"How *noble* of you!"

"Damnation," roared Nigel. Then he dragged Sylvia into his arms and kissed her.

214

"Should've done that a long time ago," Lord Raven approved.

Elisande turned away her head. "We should not be spying on them like this."

"They wouldn't thank us for making our presence known right now," Lord Raven pointed out. "Anyway, it seems that all's well that ends well."

There was the sound of a deep sigh. "Oh, *Nigel*," Sylvia Hanard murmured. "I do love you so much."

"I adore you."

"You had better, for I will never let you go again. Papa cannot make any objection to your suit after what his wife has done. Poor Papa. I feel sorry for him."

"So do I," Lord Raven agreed, as the two lovers drifted further down the Cliff Path. "I also feel a twinge of compassion for your brother, Elisande. *His* life is definitely not going to be peaceful."

"I am persuaded that you are right. But Sylvia has many good qualities, too. She is loyal and warmhearted, and though she likes to be dramatic, I think she can also be generous." Elisande smiled at some blissful inner vision. "I believe that Nigel will be happy."

"Which brings me to something I have been trying to say for the past half hour," Lord Raven said. He caught Elisande's hands and kissed them. "I am not the one to criticize the fair Sylvia since I'm also opinionated, stubborn, and hard to live with. Life with *me* would not be easy at all. Or peaceful."

"I am not used to an easy life." Elisande's heart had begun to beat more quickly. "I would not know what to do with peace and quiet."

Before Elisande could continue, there was a scraping, scrabbling step behind them and the sound of the colonel's voice. "Gone," they could hear him muttering. "God above me, she's gone."

Elisande and Lord Raven turned to see Colonel

Hanard appear around the rocks, and Elisande nearly cried out at the change in him. He was as pale as whey, and his eyes seemed to be staring into some corner of hell. Bloodless lips formed an almost inaudible word.

"Gone?" Lord Raven repeated incredulously. "You mean both of them have escaped?"

"Your groom and Redding's batman have taken the man into custody, but my wife got away."

Elisande saw an odd expression cross Lord Raven's face as the colonel reported, "I followed my wife onto the beach and to the pier where I found her offering the captain of the boat her jewels to take her away to France. I tried to stop her—eh?—but she pushed me and I slipped on the sand and fell down. That's when she got away."

As he was speaking, Nigel and Sylvia came hurrying back toward the cliffs. "Now that wicked woman will never give evidence to clear Nigel's name," Sylvia wailed.

"No need for that. All of us heard her confession when her ruffians were about to push you to your death," Lord Raven answered. "Also, we have her henchmen. They'll testify to the truth, believe me. Nigel has nothing to worry about."

"That's another matter entirely." Drawing himself to his full height, the colonel turned to the man whom he had labeled a traitor. "Redding," he grated. "I swear to you that I never suspected. Eh? Not for one moment. I thought my—my wife was above reproach."

"His rose without a thorn," Elisande heard Lord Raven murmur.

She looked anxiously at her brother as the colonel continued in a voice that was harsh with pain. "I owe you much more than an apology, sir. Eh? I'm prepared to offer you the satisfaction of a gentleman if that's your desire."

Nigel looked horrified. "Oh God, sir, no!" he exclaimed. "The only satisfaction I wanted was to clear my name. I am truly sorry for your trouble."

The colonel extended a shaking hand, and Nigel caught and pressed it. Then, his shoulders bowed, Hanard walked past the others down the Cliff Path. With a little sob, Sylvia hurried after her father and put her arms around him. Nigel followed.

Elisande murmured, "Poor man. Did he really try to stop his wife, I wonder?"

"You had the same thought, did you? I don't know the answer, but I do know what I would have done if I were in his shoes." Lord Raven's deep voice held an unusually sympathetic note as he added, "I know that even if you had done what Anabelle Hanard had done, I would have given my life to save yours. And my honor, too."

He turned back to Elisande and once again took hold of her hands. "Which brings me to that question again. Miss Redding, will you do me the honor of marrying me?"

Yes, Elisande's heart exulted. But now came a belated and unwanted resurgence of the voice of her reason. *Lord Raven is a man of the world,* it whispered. *How long do you expect to hold his love?*

"Are you sure?" she asked, and when he nodded, searched his face for answers to all her doubts. "Ivo, you know the world so much better than I. You have a fortune while I have not. Believe me, I don't want to hold you back."

"But how could you? We are kindred souls, Elisande," Lord Raven said. "Together we can venture anywhere, do anything we choose." Then he added, "But perhaps I'm wrong. After today's excitement, you may want to settle down somewhere—near your brother, perhaps, or on my Scottish estates where you'd be close to your cousin."

"And if that is the case?" Elisande queried softly.

"Then, so be it. With you I would be happy anywhere in the world. It's truly as simple as that."

He smiled at her without a trace of hesitation or self-sacrifice, and she smiled back with her heart in her clear, golden eyes—smiled so irresistibly that Raven could not bear even the small distance between them.

"Someday I would like to settle down and live in Sussex or in Scotland—but not yet." Elisande drew a happy sigh as Lord Raven put his arms around her and drew her close. "Let Con and Wigram enjoy their life of contentment, but as for us—oh, Ivo, there is a *world* out there for us to share!"